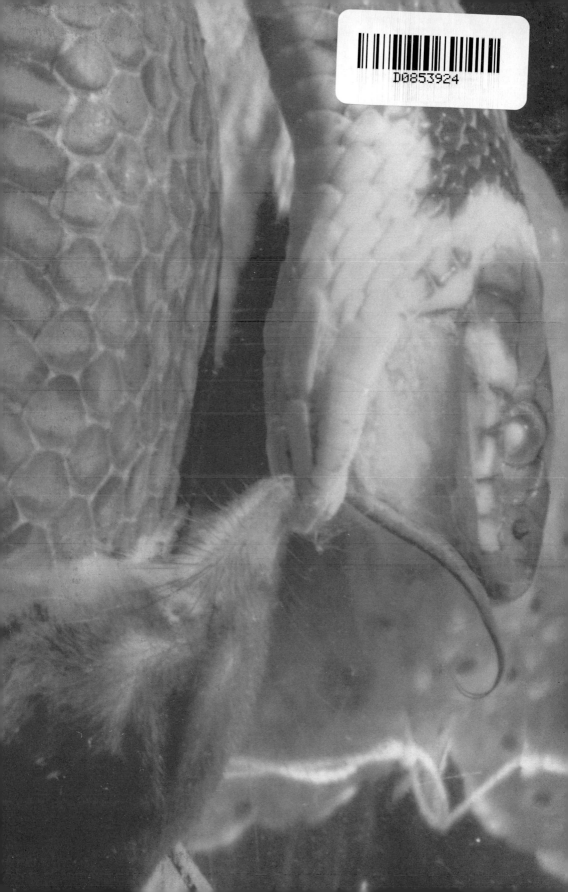

THE COMPLETE
Butcher's Tales

BOOKS BY RIKKI DUCORNET

NOVELS

The Stain
Entering Fire
The Fountains of Neptune
The Jade Cabinet

POETRY

From the Star Chamber
Wild Geraniums
Weird Sisters
Knife Notebook
The Illustrated Universe
The Cult of Seizure

CHILDREN'S BOOKS

The Blue Bird
Shazira Shazam and the Devil

Rikki Ducornet

THE COMPLETE
Butcher's Tales

Dalkey Archive Press

©1994 by Rikki Ducornet
First Edition, April 1994

ShortStory Index 1994-1998

Some of these stories first appeared in the following magazines: *The New Censorship, In This Corner, Passion, Fiction International, Iowa Review, Grain, The Canadian Fiction Magazine, Dream Scissors, Phases, Soror, Ellebore, Margin, City Lights Review, Chicago Review, Witness, Exquiste Corpse, Arsenal, Cultural Correspondence, Radical America, Mundus Artium, La Domaine internationale du surréalisme, Other Times, Uroboros,* and *Marvelous Freedom—Vigilance of Desire* (catalogue of the World Surrealist Exhibition, Chicago, 1979).

Individual tales have been anthologized in *Surrealist Stories* (Daedalus, 1994), *High Risk* (New American Library, 1993), *Hard Times* (Mercury Press, 1992), *Shoes and Shit* (Aya Press, 1984), *Contemporary Surrealist Prose* (Intermedia, 1974), and *The Stonewall Anthology of Short Fiction* (Stonewall Press, 1973).

Some of the tales appeared (often in earlier form) in previous books by Rikki Ducornet: *The Butcher's Tales* (Atlas Press, 1992), *The Volatilized Ceiling of Baron Munodi* (La Compagnie des Indes Oniriques, 1991), *Haddock's Eyes* (Les Editions du Forneau, 1987), *The Butcher's Tales* (Aya Press, 1980), and *From the Star Chamber* (Fiddlehead, 1974).

Library of Congress Cataloging-in-Publication Data
Ducornet, Rikki, 1943-
   The complete butcher's tales / Rikki Ducornet. —1st ed.
   Expanded and rev. ed. of: The butcher's tales. 1980.
   1. Fantastic fiction, America. I. Ducornet, Rikki, 1943-   Butcher's tales. II.
Title.
PSS3554.U279C66   1994   813'.54—dc20   93-36127
ISBN 1-56478-043-0

Partially funded by grants from the National Endowment for the Arts and the Illinois Arts Council.

Dalkey Archive Press
4241 Illinois State University
Normal, IL 61790-4241

Printed on permanent/durable acid-free paper and bound in the United States of America.

To Jean-Yves

Contents

Then a scream, shrill and high, rent the shuddering sky,
   And they knew that some danger was near:
The Beaver turned pale to the tip of its tail,
   And even the Butcher felt queer.

—Lewis Carroll, *The Hunting of the Snark*

THE COMPLETE
Butcher's Tales

The Volatilized Ceiling of Baron Munodi

for Pierre and Agnès Laurendeau

T he museums of Europe keep curious portraits illustrating
the assumption that the body gives the soul its shape. Da
Vinci imagined a woman with a monkey's face, Rubens human
lions, Della Porta a man with the profile of a ram. I myself am
albino; I look like an angel and so inspire acute passions. Longing for a purifying fire, men would defile me, or, taking pleasure, be absolved of sin. If I have never shared their fevers, it is
because a woman has stolen my heart. Black and clairvoyant,
she claims that one day the world will shrivel in the sun like a
plum. However, this is not the story of our love affair, but of an
obsession justified by my friend's bleak vision. Like my love for
her, it has withstood the teeth of time.

※

One evening in the early 1700s and shortly before the tragedy
which was to deny the promise of Eden, the Baron Munodi described for his little son those metal mirrors made of four isos-
celes triangles once cherished by the Greeks. At the point where
the triangles converged reigned a sacred and a potent (and po-
tentially dangerous) conjunction: here air was transformed to
fire.

Later, in lieu of a bedtime story, the Baron took his son to see
the temporary workshops installed in the arcades and galleries
of a new palace near Naples. Little Gustavo had heard of the
workshops, everybody had, and his curiosity could be contained no longer. Over ten thousand pieces destined to be incor-
porated into the geodesic marquetry of the ceilings were in the
process of being conceived, cut, painted, and dusted with gold.

3

The child perceived the workshops through a refractive fog; the air was saturated with particulated gold and he was dazzled.

Baron Munodi told Gustavo that because of their beauty and the knowledge they conveyed, the paintings were deemed evil by a repugnant authority he did not choose to name, but which wielded a tragic power.

"Some believe that these images can make beasts talk," the Baron told his son, "in the manner of the serpent which tempted Eve; and that I have the power to excite tempests." If it is true that the Baron was powerful, his power, like the ceiling which blossomed in the torchlight, oscillated on the verge of an abyss.

With eager eyes Gustavo devoured green lions and gravid elephants, a submerged city of mermen shining beneath the moon, a laughing cupid, a man with the face of a camel, a girl as naked as a lily. From out of a blue oval the size and color of a puffin's egg, a one-eyed sun gazed at him with such urgency that he blushed before he looked away. Then, peering around a smocked and spattered elbow, the boy saw an image which vibrated so mysteriously that he was not content to touch it, but must lick it with his tongue and, putting it to his quivering nostrils, deeply inhale.

This potent picture imprinted itself not only on the child's brain, but upon the imaginations of future generations. I have awakened from startling dreams which reveal to me just what was now being revealed to Gustavo:

A mature albino ape, its heart pierced by an arrow, falls from a tropical tree. As he falls he attempts to catch the bloody ropes spouting from his breast. In truth his wound is fathomless, a mortal fracture in the body of the world. Gustavo sees that the ape's hands are very like his own.

As in the swelter of torchlight Gustavo gazed enamored of the ape, the image was gently taken from him and the cipher 666 painted on the back. Then it was set down among many hundreds of others which lay scattered in the manner of the zodiacs which animate the vaults of Heaven. Soon the features of the room and the painters' faces dissolved in a vortex as red as the wings of angels: a swarm of apprentices had descended upon a freshly varnished set of pictures to dust them with gold.

That night a conflagration raged throughout the Baron's workshops. By morning all that remained of the palace was char, and of the painters a fistful of calcinated teeth. The ten thousand images were reduced to smoke; the secret of Baron Munodi's ceiling had volatilized.

Proof of the catastrophe's perfidious nature, the Baron was found assassinated, his heart pierced by a long nail with such force that his body was secured to the boards of his bed. Awakening drenched in her beloved's blood, the Baroness—whose lucidity was legendary—was bound and carried off as one possessed to a madhouse. There she gave birth to my ancestor who, I know from one famous portrait in the Prado, I do not resemble. Gustavo died before reaching maturity; I, sole heir to the Munodi line and memory, am childless. A friend who knows such things has told me that this explains my compulsion to capture what I can in black ink on white paper.

✻

Baron Munodi's properties and his little son Gustavo were seized by the executive officers of the Inquisition. After an exhaustive search, a pentagon was found freshly painted in an attic, and among the Baron's things a ball of feathers and a shoe studded with pins. A globe was found also, and a map of the heavens that showed the planets in orbit.

Gustavo was stripped of his silk shirt and dressed in a penitent's shift of sacking. The vivid curls of his infancy were shorn from his head, and he was forced to spend the lion's part of his days among God-fearing arsonists in prayer.

As he had neither pastimes nor companions to ease the morbid placidity of monastic life, Gustavo courted vertigo in the shape of a memory. From incessant practice he could within an instant conjure the ape and carry it perpetually before him. Image 666 was his own elementary secret, the exact center of his mind's incarnate mirror. Try as they did to discover the exact nature of the umbilicus that joined Gustavo to his past, his father's assassins had to admit to failure.

The monks explained to the Grand Inquisitor that they did

not know the object of the child's worship and so could not subvert it. They knew only that it was an alien practice. The heresiarch's own son was prey to an incomprehensible exultation which had nothing to do with Jesus Christ; his fervent prayers were all his own. No one knew that as the others fixed the cross, Gustavo gazed inward upon that image of the ape which was Baron Munodi's metaphor for loss, dolorous spiritual mishap and detour, and a primary element in a vast, coded message of incendiary significance. Just as the Baron's enemies feared, the ceiling was no idle inventory, but the revelation of an itinerary. Now as I write this, as the very atmosphere escapes into sidereal space and the world's balloon deflates, I fear its vanished alphabets spelled out *the only itinerary*. Gustavo had seen the unassembled pages of the Book of Salvation. Envy, greed, and groundless fear had destroyed it.

✳

One rare afternoon of peace in the monastery gardens, Gustavo chanced to witness a bitter argument about the nature of the creature evoked in chapter thirteen of John's Apocalypse which reads: *May he who is intelligent calculate the number of the beast. The number is that of a man, and his number is six hundred and sixty-six.*

Delirious with joy, Gustavo ran to the circle of contentious monks and cried out:

"I know! For I have seen it! And see him even now! He is an ape! Oh! A beautiful ape!"

Lifted into the air by an ear, Gustavo received such a slap that the ear was nearly torn from his head. Then he was kicked down corridors of stone and thrust into a cell, windowless but for a vertical aperture just wide enough to send an arrow into the heart of the forest.

From that time on Gustavo, in concordance with the *Instructio,* was struck each night to hammer the cruel nail of piety deep into his skull, and again at daybreak to banish whatever fancy might have slipped down his festering ear as he slept. It was said that the Baron's son could not be saved, not even by an extraordinary act of grace, that his words had divulged an unforgivable heresy:

"The child," the monks informed the Grand Inquisitor, "implies that the Son of God is an ape."

What the assessors, councillors, and judges of the Inquisition reviled as a crime of *lèse-majesté divine*, is today, except within the most reactionary enclaves of the Middle East, North Africa, and North America, common knowledge. The exemplary science of genetics has corroborated the marvel: the ape's number —give or take a chromosome or two—is the mirror of man's.

Once vigorous, a boy who delighted in pictures of the rope-dancing elephants of Rome and Pompeian acrobats, Gustavo was now but bone and nerve, subject to visions of subterranean demons. His ravaged face refused to mend and a mortal fever gnawed at his mind. He did not notice the crusted iron cross which hung suspended from a nail, threatening, at any instant, to shatter his skull. As a moon the ape had risen, and it orbited his thoughts. I who have shadowed gorillas with the hope that the quintessential nature of my ancestry be revealed to me, understand that infant's *idée fixe*: it is my own. You see, I have inherited my purpose from a child dead over two hundred years. Some spontaneous influence, perhaps electric, has caused all the Munodis to share Gustavo's obsession: my great-grand-father spent a lifetime investigating the footprints of the *Yeti*; my father's father lived among the *Macaca speciosa* of Thailand; my great-aunt Dolorosa, when she was not tracking baboons, wrote an excellent book on Rosalie-Zaccharie Ferriol—the ravishing French albino (and according to a precious engraving, my doppelgänger), whose celebrated eyes burned so brightly they pierced the hearts of everyone who saw her; and an essay on *Moby-Dick* in which she notes that unlike white apes, white whales are common (or, rather, *were* common; whales of any color are no longer common).

✳

It is now time to return to Gustavo who is dying, and who dreams he is once again in the Baron's workshops. In the light of resinous torches, apprentices run up and down the mazed avenues of the painters' tables, seeding the puissant images with gold. The air is so charged with gold that when Gustavo opens his eyes for the last time he sees that his dream's luminescence has flooded his cell, that he is held in the tender embrace of the beloved ape. An angel exiled from Heaven, it has fallen onto his verminous pallet of straw.

When the monks find Gustavo's body, they burn it. It is written in their erroneous books that a toad hopped from the flames and that a viper circled the pyre. These are fables. The truth is that a morbid agitation disrupted the questionable peace of that wicked place thereafter and led to its decline.

✳

My own researches into albinism and, inevitably, melanism, have taken me to the far reaches of this our shrinking planet and evolved into a study of the coded alphabets which are visible on the backs and faces of all the beasts of the animal kingdom. Above the fortieth north parallel I have, in months of incessant night, tracked white wolves and blue foxes. In the smoky depths of forests on fire I have seen hermaphrodite snakes of ink and milk, their eyes the color of the caviar of scallops and so rare they can be counted on the fingers of one hand.

Recovering from malarial fever in France I have recorded the white spots on the backs of piebald crows (*turdus merula*), which, having beaked the tainted waters, plummet from the pollarded trees. I have spent an entire decade mapping the markings of capricorn beetles and even the ears of tigers; their seed is crippled irretrievably. Just as the whales, the apes, and Baron Munodi's miraculous ceiling, they too shall vanish.

✳

Recently, as I lay beside my mistress, I dreamed a disturbing dream: I had bought several pounds of fresh squid to prepare for many illustrious friends, all who had, miraculously, survived the gas chambers. The squid were slippery and wet, and like any inspired intuition, hard to hold. They were also perfectly white. I took each up one by one and with a very sharp knife slit them open, revealing a perfect little figure of a man, white as ivory and dressed like the princes of ancient Persia—studded turbans on their heads and scimitars in their belts. They wore neatly buttoned vests, and one had caviar—tiny white pearls of it—clinging to his loins and inner thighs.

With care I slipped each perfect man from his casing of flesh and severed the head. Then I cut the arms from the torso, and after that the legs. I feared they would waken and scream, but all slept and if one bled, his blood was pale, hardly blood at all: the blood of a fish. When I had finished I realized with a shudder that there had been 111 manikins, and that I had sliced each one into six.

I have described this dream to a psychoanalyst, a philosopher, and to my mistress.

The psychoanalyst insists that the squid is the symbol of the penis, the sleeping man I would kill rather than arouse. The philosopher suggests that these mermen are the metaphor for the soul's longing for gnosis which the mind assassinates from fear —grace more terrible to the uninformed heart than eternal darkness. I believe that my mistress's answer is by far the most satisfactory, although I know that all answers are fragments in the puzzle of the True:

"The dismembering of the body symbolizes its dissolution, the first step towards regeneration, and without which resurrection is impossible. The water that spills from the squid's body, like the blood from the heart of the wounded ape, symbolizes the amniotic fluid, and above all the primal waters from which all things descend: green algae, blue foxes, men and women both white and black."

＊

The years pass too swiftly. Like a fantastic doctrine become ashes before it can be read, my lover and I will be reduced to dust. In one brief lifetime, I cannot undo the tragic loss of a child's life, nor begin to reconstruct an alchemical lexicon; nor can I, with exactitude, chart a family tree. Even the finite combinations on the backs of common beetles elude me. Yet I am certain that should the world survive, others will be haunted in much the same way and dream similar dreams. This is my greatest hope, if Eden is to be one day reconstituted.

Mademoiselle Clistore in Cairo

M ademoiselle Clistore taught the Feminine Arts at the Osiris Academy in Cairo, Egypt, from 1945 to 1954—the year of her hushed dismissal, the bitter pill of illness and death.

For three hours each Monday afternoon, the daughters of the Nile, dressed in dung-colored cloth and Oxford ties, labored single pieces of foxed drawing paper.

Embroidery claimed Tuesdays. With the drear belligerence of sand beaching monumental sphinxes, sheets and pillow slips accumulated in Clistore's cupboard.

The girls sewed with red thread and often pricked their fingers, tainting the pure white linen with blood. Still reeling with the perplexities of menses, these stains caused them to blush with shame—and fear: Mademoiselle Clistore, very like the Countess Bathory someone's older brother had had the luck to catch at Cheops Cinema, punished severely. Eyes red and fingers stinging, the careless lass would be kept after class to embroider her crime:

> On this day, the fourth of May
> Having pricked my finger XX
> I am justly punished XXXXXX
> Shaza Ahmed XXXXXXXXXXX
> La ilaha illa- 'llah XXXXXXXX
> XXXXXXXXXXXXXXXXXXXXX

(no God but Allah)—the whole underlined with a row of scarlet Xs. To make matters worse, Mademoiselle Clistore, having left her native Dijon many years before but having brought with her intact the French attitudes, would seize the trembling mud of the virgin's shoulder, and flesh, like linen, would be marked with a red signature.

In truth, Mademoiselle Clistore hated sewing. Hated the silly baskets, the pointless needles. A trained nurse, the Second World War had given her countless opportunities to administer heartily to the buttocks of comatose soldiers.

Sewing she had left to the surgeon, a morose and corpulent major named Félix Potin (a distant relation to the grocery baron) who seduced her in a makeshift lavatory and who had had the cheek to request she shave off all her pubic hair prior to their next encounter. Quite suddenly the war ended, so suddenly she wondered if the loss of her integrity had in some uncanny way precipitated the Allied invasion of Normandy. In the ensuing bustle she never did encounter Félix again, but on the advice of a horoscope (Clistore was a Bull in the House of Venus) and a magician named Flavia, took a ship from Marseilles to Alexandria.

The Fertile Crescent appealed to her at once. She liked the peculiar vegetation, the men squatting in dresses, the women camouflaged beneath heaps of dusty black sacking. She liked to sit on swept terraces eating the flesh of chickens fattened on almonds and milk, to sleep beneath the eye of a pyramid.

The Moslem call to prayer thrilled her with its eerie urgency. On a visit to the south she marveled at the tattooed Bedouins, their houses of hair and tasselated camels. As she wrote to Flavia, she had come to see herself as a Bedouin, tenacious and enduring. She dieted, engaging upon a ruthless quest for self-desiccation. Taking inspiration from "these dusty latitudes," she yearned to become "dry, manly, hard, unyielding—a creature of sinew, nerve and bone." And although her pubic hair had, after much discomfort, grown back, she paid to have every last bit of it pulled out again by a strange withered creature in bangles who performed this tedious task with great quantities of hot caramel.

Mademoiselle was large, European and therefore (and for the first time in her life) *visible*. In the small circle of self-imposed exiles she quickly cut herself a slice. She had a certain seductive erudition; she entertained a genuine fascination for the early Gnostic books of Fayoum—all for the most part incoherent— and her conversation waxed with veils, "pro-triple spirits," and left-handed doors. As her acquaintances were starved for any queerness whatsoever, she was—up until the scandal—an appreciated teatime companion.

She never mastered Arabic, but volubly admired a language that boasts over one thousand words for camel. Her English was presentable, if irregular, and within three weeks she had landed the job at Osiris Academy, the previous Sewing Mistress —in imitation of the Pharaoh Menes—having been trampled to death by a hippopotamus. Now it is rumored that the company of all those young girls titillated a latent appetite for authority.

Mademoiselle was upright, strict, and autonomous, her personal life impeccable (indeed she had none); she dressed with the sobriety of mummia and never laughed. And if her punishments were a trifle fanciful, no one at the Academy seemed to care. They were Mademoiselle's only eccentricity and after all, she was French.

*

Tenure of office assured, Mademoiselle Clistore regarded her pupils as legitimate victims. They were Muslims, and Islam—as she wrote to Flavia—"teaches total submission and surrender to a Greater Will." Her pupils all came from reactionary, well-to-do families.

"These Semites," Mademoiselle Clistore insisted in a letter to the magician, "are not Jews." She had developed her own theory about racial purity. "These Egyptians are True Semites, due to isolation and the uniformity of life in the Saharan wilderness. My little pupils are all Scheherazades. Each boasts two black ones—and I am referring not to water and dates but to eyes and hair. My favorite, Shaza, has a mole behind her knee— very like a drop of ambergris upon an alabaster dish."

Along with the Feminine Arts, Osiris Academy taught English grammar and history, how to boil mutton, and simple mathematics. Daily by the frankincense the pupils played volleyball, the only sport allowed them—except during their menses when they were expected to remain seated in the library to memorize, with the help of a badly bruised dictionary, Latin phrases: *deus ex machina; ad nauseum.* The girls did not study their own history; Egyptian history was considered disgraceful by their fathers and Osiris alike. Religious issues were discussed but once: when that ill-fated fez-fitter from Zamalik complained that Shaza Ahmed, his betrothed, had, during the Ramadan recess, shown her future mother-in-law pastels of the infant Christ surrounded by asses and cows. Mademoiselle was called into the office of the Headmistress where apparently unmoved she reminded the haberdasher (who in fact she hated on sight as a rival) that the Christ's many miraculous deeds—the manufacture of clay birds and coherent conversation in the cradle—are recorded with wonderment in the Koran itself.

It is said that the Sewing Mistress blushed deeply when the Head suggested that the crèche figure (which she had bought with her own money in the Mouski from a leper who sold miscellanea when he was not pulling teeth) be replaced by a plaster cast of a severed foot, a faience fig dish, and nine dried gourds. To prove her independence, if only to herself, Mademoiselle Clistore had her pupils copy a magazine illustration from *Paris-Match* of a black and a white Scottish terrier sitting together on a blue armchair. None of her pupils ever managed to render the chair's proportions convincingly. Mademoiselle's bitter mood worsened.

✳

The scandal had not yet subsided when Mademoiselle Clistore was dead of a liver ailment unheard of on the continent. When Flavia described her friend's symptoms to a doctor, he could only look away in embarrassment and shake his head in disbelief. As specified in her will, a rare copy of Mr. Horner's 1924 English translation of the *Pistis Sophia* was sent to Flavia; ever since the magician's quiet life has been perturbed by those many weird mysteries.

The Imaginary Infancy of Heinrich Schliemann

When Heinrich Schliemann was three years old, he stooped to seize a small rusty key from the street and was told by his father, a man of circumstance wearing a windbreaker, never to pick up anything from the ground.

"For," Herr Schliemann pontificates with an emphatic gesture of the forefinger, "who knows if a dog has not at one time or another done some business there."

Indeed, the little Heinrich has often watched dogs gambol in the park, nosing out one another's acquaintance and doing business with admirable frequency. And previously, as he had paused beside an unusually complexioned pebble, he had seen a day nurse crouch furtively behind a perambulator. And yet (what man can safely say he knows the secrets of his own son's heart?) as Heinrich Schliemann's papa turns his head away and continues his stroll, leaving his small son to toddle obediently after, Heinie spies a coin blazing in the sun and, with a pickpocket's nimbleness, pops it into his mouth.

＊

Heinie explores the surface of the coin with his tongue. It tastes of treason, of uncooked liver and enchantment. It brings to mind the dramatic drypoint engravings he has glimpsed beneath their veils of tissue paper in the forbidden sepulcher of his papa's study: scenes of sirens perched on shell-crusted pinnacles, of woods bristling with boars, the flaming citadel of Troy.

He thinks: *The coin is mine. Papa will never know about it.* Heinie knows the dangers of his mother's liverish looks and worse, the cracking terror of Herr Schliemann's paddle. His papa has told him what is done to thieves and spies in Arabia, and has warned him:

15

"Should I ever catch you thieving or spying, I'll cut off your hands myself."

✳

Heinie steals a look through the crack in the wall of the family mausoleum. Upon the tombs of his ancestors he admires the Angora cats—Helen and Paris—so beloved of his great-grand-mother. Their white marble likenesses coil upon a sarcophagus of porphyry. Unfortunately, he is seen.

Heinie's papa takes the paddle down from its hook. Little Heinie tastes of its exemplary rigor with all his heart and soul, although he has, upon his knees, implored mercy, and when that fails, does his best to scuffle under his mother's vanity where he is at once trapped like a toad beneath a brick.

In his humiliation, Heinie eats a mud of dust and tears.

✳

And now, all at once, remembering how his spirit and body have been violated, Heinie is seized in terror's fist. Trembling for his very soul, he delivers up the coin.

It is gold. Herr Schliemann sees it at once burning in the thin puddle of his son's mortification. As Heinie's buttocks catch fire, his father liberates the coin with a stick, wipes it off with his handkerchief, and pockets it. But he does not threaten to cut off Heinie's hands. Instead, he gazes upon his son with satisfaction.

Herr Schliemann believes in God; that is to say, he often asks God for favors. And that very morning, he had asked to be granted the boon of an inkling—no matter how small—of his son's destiny.

✳

That night, long after Heinie has been tucked away in his little bed, Herr Schliemann strokes his wife's breasts beneath the linen nightgown which has been in the family for three generations.

16

"Today in the park," he whispers, pawing gently at the cloth, "our Heinrich's future was revealed to me!" Like the head of a turtle, his wife's heart bolts beneath his hand.

Herr Schliemann has a propensity for drama. He says no more, but just as he breaks his rolls into two before spreading them with butter, he parts his wife's thighs and, brandishing his rosy staff with its sputtering head and full, russet-bearded cheeks, penetrates her with the firm conviction of a man claiming his own.

"A . . . a banker!" he gasps. "Our Heinie . . . will be . . . a [*snort!*] BANKER!"

Once her husband falls asleep, Heinie's mama slips from the eiderdowns to descend the stairs and with brimming eyes reflect upon her son's sleeping face. For day after day, as she has sat by the fire embroidering the Acropolis upon her husband's slippers with yellow thread, she has prayed for something grander, more enduring. And in daydreams she has seen Heinrich Schliemann her son accomplishing great feats of the imagination: deciphering the Rosetta Stone, painting the portrait of Whistler's mother, engineering the Suez Canal, the Eiffel Tower, inventing the microscope. . . .

Haddock's Eyes

Borges, Uqbar's most celebrated chronicler (and I drink his noble health), aware of my consuming weakness for early Gnostic curios, suggested I "join the digs" at the islands of Axa Delta (and in particular, Smerdis) where gems embossed with the head of Cronos have been unearthed in quantity.

It is most unfortunate that before these objects disappeared, they were neither numbered nor charted. As Walter Bongo, the regretted director of the Smerdic Service of Antiquities, explained in a letter, incomplete descriptions of those dramatic exhumations were available until only very recently when, as obstinate ill luck would have it, they were unwittingly thrown out with the trash.

Before I mislaid Walter's correspondence, I committed it to memory. This scrupulous bureaucrat, inspired scientist, and much-lamented friend explained that the gems "trickled through the sands like water through a sieve; it was rather like hunting for haddock's eyes."

Walter wrote of another astonishing discovery. In 1903, La Belle Otéro and her lover Hans were looking for the faerie gems, when the ground gave way beneath their feet and a somber head, hideously pocked by unfathomable antiquity, was recovered from the heather.

Due to a curious accumulation of circumstances, I was able to procure a nearly intact photograph of the star upon the site, wearing white and standing in relief against the celebrated pewter of the Tlönic sky. Mute laughter plays upon those divine lips, but her eyes are cloudy with foreboding, as well they might. In sixty minutes the head will pierce the air with a savage cry and, like flesh upon fire, quite melt away.

✳

The diggings at Smerdis are subject to vicissitudes great and small. If, when the head self-destructed, the deception of the international scholarly community was boundless, there are those who insist that the head never existed and, like those "haddock's eyes," was nothing more than "the collective hallucination of a spoiled, bored, sophisticated leisure class." And if it is true that La Belle Otéro (who was, in fact, exceedingly plain) seemed herself to profit from that as-yet inexplicable phenomenon, the rude journalist who penned these needlessly cruel remarks was in the pay of Walter's lifelong rival Piaster Camel, the unscrupulous curator of the Coptic Museum. However, my task is not to describe the odious maneuvers of a rival clan, but to faithfully transcribe the process of a highly precarious archeological inquiry, knowing full well that when the excitement is over, these fragile pages will, like butterflies in wheat, crumble into oblivion.

✳

Before he passed away, Walter begged to see the photograph—proof that the head, however briefly, was not a fantastic dream but a reality. Well aware that Walter was swiftly waning, I never did tell him the truth.

It goes without saying, I have examined the photograph with the greatest attentiveness. A somber mass *is* visible in the rubble beside the singer's feet. But it is featureless and could be almost anything at all—a battered melon, a clod of decomposing rock, a sophisticate's hat. Like La Belle Otéro's overrated voice, the head has left no material trace. It exists only as long as men choose to remember it.

✳

My own forays into the grassy knolls of Smerdis have been more fruitful. As I waded in the dissolved soprano's footsteps, I found a small but exceedingly heavy cone, an *ur*—just as Borges describes in his monograph: "Tlön, Uqbar, Orbis Tertius."

19

When the cone is placed upon a perfectly flat surface it commences to tick, like a clock, or a live crab in a tub of water. It also has an undeniable propensity to attract serpents that coil about its glassy surface like cats in heat. Indeed, as long as the cone was in my possession, I was greatly inconvenienced. So much so, I happily ceded it to the Brooklyn-Basil Institute for Tlönic Studies in Berlin.

According to *The Book of Crimes,* he who knows how to listen to the cone's ticking will recognize *the dismal murmur of the human emotions, the thrilling history of the mutations of the human spirit in space-time and the secrets of the fructifications of all things.* Needless to say, the Gnostics of Smerdis were worshipers of sexual extravagance and it is my conviction that the head the actress unwittingly kicked, diabolically horned and lipped, was that of Ialdaboath himself. And that Ialdaboath, Cronos, and the Snake are all emanations of the First Principle—nothing less than the three faces of the One God.

✳

It is no secret that La Belle Otéro and her lover fought bitterly during their brief holiday; Hans did not share his mistress's enthusiasm for dervishes and national dishes. (Perhaps I should advise the budding enthusiast of Tlön that barley germ broiled in rancid dromedary ghee is, like raw batter, an acquired taste. And that the deceptions inherent in Smerdic archeology are inevitable.)

Hans, the singer's luggage, her car, her cash, and what is worse, her voice, vanished. Few who know the country blame the man; most blame the clime: the molten sky's cyclopean eye, the treacherous sands, and most of all, that mysterious corrosive influence that causes havoc—not only among the uninitiated, but within a diminishing scholarly community as well. For the excavators at Axa Delta are the most careless I have ever encountered: their diggings are cluttered with luncheon refuse, their charts shamelessly pawed and spotted with bloody ink, the precious artifacts—all too rare—pocked, smashed, and misnumbered (when they are not missing altogether).

Like all men of science, I am subject to wind, the perambulations of the moon, the constellations, and anxiety. I regret to add that I lied to Walter and that after his death, not to become a laughingstock (and jeopardize my inquiry and simultaneously sully Walter's memory), I destroyed the photograph. For you see, the more I scrutinized that blob in the sand at the singer's feet, the more convinced I became that it was anything but a head.

Friendship

Felix did not notice when the bump first appeared just above his left ear. Nor much later, when it had grown to the size of a lima bean. But when it had attained the size and consistency of an unripe plum, his wife saw it and asked him what in the name of Mary it was.

"I don't know," Felix replied. He was angry with himself because she had seen it first. She was always the first to see things —like the day the doorknob had fallen off and the bird had died. She had seen the mouse, the burn on his best jacket, the roach nest.

"You have no idea," she said, "but I do. It is a tumor, as sure as Dickey lies as dead as a doorknob. And if I was you I'd see a doctor, before it swells up and carries you off to another world. Seeing how you ain't exactly on this one, not noticing the thing —big as a goddamned hot-air balloon."

Felix made an appointment to see the doctor, who was not in and very busy and would not be free until the month after next —could it wait?

"It can wait!" his wife cried after Felix had hung up. "It's only a goddamned malignancy for Christ's sake—who the hell do they think they're pushing around? If the goddamned pope woke up with a pink dirigible stuck to his ear, they'd have him under in five minutes!"

"Anesthetic?" Felix pondered. "Then it's serious?"

*

Two months later the doctor was prodding Felix's prominence. It had grown to the size of a grapefruit. "Best not to touch it," the doctor said, squeezing. "Wear this brace, of my own design." He handed Felix a flesh-colored device that slipped over the ears and was adjustable. "I wouldn't worry," he added, "unless there is real pain."

There was no pain. Felix went about his business. The brace proved so comfortable he forgot about the tuberosity. His wife did not. Felix awoke one morning to find her reaching for it.

"I wonder what color it is?" she said.

Felix, surprising them both, said: "No. It is mine." It was the first time in their life together that he had called anything his own.

✳

That Christmas, Felix stood alone in the bathroom in front of the medicine-closet mirror. His wife was gone; he supposed she was living with her mother. His own mother, thank God, was dead. Slowly he undid the brace, which was at the point of bursting at the seams. He had the odd conviction that it was no longer necessary, that the bump had attained a certain buoyancy. Gently he undid the back catch and slipped the straps from his ears.

In the mirror Felix saw that the growth had a face. It was not a tumor at all, but a fine head, very much like his own—if a good deal younger. A pleasant head, bald, companionable; a head which, if you passed it in the street, would make you think: "What an agreeable-looking fellow!"

The head, which had been watching Felix very closely all the while, saw the happy expression on Felix's face, saw the look of mild surprise transform itself to pride, and pride to friendliness. This pleased the new head, made it at once grateful and joyous. It smiled, showing as it did a handsome set of pearly teeth.

"Welcome!" said Felix. "Please feel at home!"

"Thank you!" said the head. "I do."

"Then there is no problem," said Felix.

"None," said the head. "So why should there be a problem?"

"I am so happy," said Felix. "I have been so alone. All those years with my wife were so very lonely. . . ."

"I know," said the head.

"Tell me you will never leave me," Felix implored softly.

"I will never leave you," the head said simply.

23

Bazar

Although a man of imagination, eager to confess his anxieties, Félibien is French. He manages what the French call a *bazar* in Constantine, Algeria, in the years prior to national independence. He sells plastic pails and metal pliers and a thousand other things besides.

Félibien believes his life has no other object but spiritual progress. Surrounded by dirt and infidels, he tries with all his might to detach his heart from sin. He carries out the duties of his state with zeal and merit, or so he thinks. And this until the stains come into his life and Amer, and Amer's brother, if not necessarily in that order.

Félibien believes in the *bazar*. By selling thermos bottles and bathing caps he thinks of himself as a fountainhead of progress. Thanks to Félibien, squalid clay vessels are being replaced by enameled colanders. Instead of bandy twigs of marshmallow, Arab babies are teething on his rubber ducklings.

It is odd that a Frenchman exulted by principles of sound moral certainty should have befriended "an ancient, atheistic American" (and the description is her own). A merchant from the Mzab had set Hattie up in a glossy, cobalt blue-and-white tiled house in the old section of the city between the mosque and the bordello, "which expresses exactly how he felt about me—a species of pious lust." The Mozabite was a bigamist whose wives frittered away their lives quarreling among the goats and babies of Ghardaïa, a blue oasis she has never seen.

In 1923, Hattie was a rebellious spinster indulging in a Mediterranean cruise. The handsome merchant, the Persian oval of his face, his carpet warehouses, the cool, spare house seduced her. Until he died she kept the pantry stocked with the pistachios he adored.

Hattie often visits the museum. The curator invites her to join him when he goes into the country to explore the Roman ruins at Tidis. There the archeological fellaheen find Hattie tremendously funny in her track shoes, sunbonnet, and scarves. And Hattie, loving, generous, and seventy, laughs with them. Her most cherished hours are those spent in the late afternoons among the splendent, baffling ruins when they all sit together sipping mint tea from scalding glasses, speaking softly, softly laughing, and passing the time-puzzled objects from hand to hand: the bent brooches and glass beads and red shards they have that very day unearthed.

Many of the objects brought to light are of a pornographic nature. The most curious of these is a bas-relief of a winged phallus strutting on two legs, an erect phallus balancing between its thighs. The fellaheen admire Hattie when she placidly disencrusts this with a camel's-hair brush. Of her they say, "She is a man."

❋

Exile makes for strange bedfellows. What does Hattie see in Félibien? His piety gets her goat. He is stuffy and hopelessly neurotic. But she adores eccentrics, loves to tease and mother him, and both are preoccupied with the problem of evil, although their vocabulary differs: he calls it sin, she tragedy. And he is lonely and Hattie has a golden heart. She thinks Félibien has never known love.

Has never known love. Only a furtive, shameful incident with a perverse little Kabil of fifteen, a misdemeanor the memory of which rises like a bubble of gas, a misdemeanor so sinful, a sinfulness so demonic, so misleading, that he always doubts he has actually committed it. And if he has, has he confessed? He cannot remember. Certainly he would have confessed to God, had there been something to confess, but has he confessed to a priest? And if not, need he? In Algeria, what he and the boy had done, *if they had done it*, is as current as loose change.

❋

Félibien: "The plebeians do not consider the *delectationes morosas* as sins. It is the same with immodest talk which they call joking."

Hattie: "Where do you pick this stuff up? *Good God!*"

Félibien: "I was once a priest."

Hattie: "Christ! A priest! Defrocked?"

Félibien: "Hm. Yes . . . yes! I suppose I was!"

Hattie: "Defrocked! Dearest Félibien, you never cease to amaze and astound and, *dearest* Félibien, amuse me! Now. *Why* were you defrocked? Confess."

Félibien: "I-I can't remember. Hattie. Truly. I can't. It's been so long."

Hattie: "A likely story. God only knows what Freud would have said to *that.* "

Félibien: "I *hate* Frudd. I'd rather you not bring him up so often."

Hattie: "Oh *do* I? Do I bring him up *so often?* But I can't escape him. And neither, darling, can you. DE-FROCKED! Think of it!"

✳

Félibien is in his forty-fourth year. He is a bony, slightly stooped man who will keep his hair, although it is very thin. His teeth, if yellow, are solid enough. He is not good-looking, yet has a boyish charm which has to do with a most painful slenderness and the way a hank of greenish hair falls over his eyes. His socks are invariably mismatched. He often forgets to sleep. He collides into people and furniture. He had wanted to be a pharmacist, but having failed his exams miserably, was ordained instead. Suddenly he was a priest no longer. When his father's brother died, Félibien, the favorite nephew, inherited the *bazar*.

✳

The *bazar* is a long tiled room with a narrow oak counter that fences off a wall laddered with shelves. It is near enough to the hotel to get the tourist trade and also at the edge of the *souks* where human traffic is thickest. Sly women in veils, their stun-

26

ning prepubescent daughters clinging shyly to their shrouds, barter for henna beside colonials clamoring for corks and irritated tourists after bug powder and maps.

Félibien has recently hired a toady, cross-eyed fellow whose job it is to fetch tea from the tearoom across the littered street, brush off the male clients' pants from knees to ankles with a stiff whisk broom, shoo away the flies, the boys, and a foul-mouthed madman who every afternoon positions himself in the street to spit into the faces of unveiled women. He also sweeps up at the end of the day and sprinkles the floor with fresh sawdust.

In fine weather Félibien hangs soccer balls out in nets, bottle brushes festoon the door, and starched orange dishrags crackle in the breeze. In the winter the door remains tightly shut and the smells of human urine and stewing tomatoes and rotting dates and donkey dung remain outside. Then the *bazar* smells of the dust that has collected over the years in the drawers of nails and bolts and screws; it smells of the waxed counter and of the grease which keeps the iron knives looking new, of the soiled bills of money Félibien keeps in a drawer under the counter beneath a cardboard box of squashed, thumb-sized dolls. The *bazar* smells of pine soap, of rat shit and mint tea. It smells of old plaster—for the place needs repair—especially the ceiling which is badly stained. And blood. No. Surely the *bazar* does not smell of blood!

Félibien likes the *bazar* best after hours when the door is locked—very late at night when the floor is spread with new sawdust and glitters like deep, still waters. Then no client disturbs his thoughts and he is alone behind the counter, sitting on his chair above the cellar trap, his feet up, a lonely helmsman facing a sea of silence: Captain Félibien sailing the night. The trusting passengers are tucked away in their berths: ducks and pails and dollies are stowed away like eggs in their dozens on the shelves behind his head, hanging from the rafters or laid low in the cellar. The moonlight sifts through the cluttered windows bathing everything in a thin veil of silver-threaded brocade, and Félibien feels a strange, sustained excitement as if he is on the verge of an important discovery: a submerged city, a rare winged phallus, or antique mosaic wall, chipped and swollen but with its glazed figures of nude wrestlers curiously intact.

27

The objects of his trade cluster around him like trusting children. At any instant the little dolls may come to life and flutter about the room like cherubim. The black crinkly hairpins lying together in their boxes could be the canned fishes of another planet and his thick sheets of writing paper the grey tundras of worlds uninhabited and one-dimensional.

Félibien loves to sit thus and dream. But the other Félibien, the daytime Félibien, fears that dreaming is self-indulgent. As he washes and dresses he accuses himself of idleness. For guilt with him is a constant practice. He is certain that to confess to a priest what Hattie calls his "nighttime follies" would be nothing short of ridiculous. He confesses his nighttime follies to Hattie, yet insists over lunch in her spacious dining room:

Félibien: "I am a pious person."

Hattie: "Yes. I know that. Félibien—you are too hard on yourself. I'd like to get a good look at your pajamas."

Félibien: "My—?"

Hattie: "Yes. To see if they are really made of horsehair. And your bed. To see if it is made of nails."

Félibien: "You are laughing at me again."

Hattie: "Of course I am! It does us both a world of good. But you must tell me now—what is it you see in the *stains?*"

Félibien does not hear her question. His mind is wandering. He is wondering: what if one confesses to a mortal sin *once* to discover later that one has in fact committed the sin *twice,* or three times say, or four! Must one confess again? What are the rules, the confounded rules? He cannot remember.

"I suppose," he says aloud, "I must confess again."

"You bet!" says Hattie. "Here's lunch!"

✳

Hattie's boy is named Amer. He has tinderbox eyes that ignite everyone they touch. Félibien would never admit it to himself but what he enjoys most about Hattie's lunches is that he may at his leisure watch the superb creature walk around the room. Right now he is admiring the boy's beautiful naked feet. Amer smells of freshly steamed couscous. Or are they having couscous for lunch?

Because Amer is in the room, Félibien begins to brag about the curious pictures he has seen in the stains on his plaster ceiling. It is a vain, prideful act and he will surely suffer for it. Félibien is very pleased with his fanciful interpretations of the stains and does multiply and embellish those enchanted grottoes and grotesque caricatures and flooded woodlands and fumaroles and bats.

"Da Vinci—" Hattie says something he does not catch because now Amer is standing beside him with a platter of stuffed pike. Félibien inhales the steamed-wheat smell of the boy's skin, his clean perfume of a freshly opened oyster. Serving himself the best part of the fish, which includes the tail because Hattie insists, he asks Amer in Arabic:

"Have *you* ever daydreamed looking at the stains in plaster?"

Amer frowns. To him the question seems somehow unforgivably indiscreet. He does not answer but stands with surly grace at Félibien's side pressing steamed vegetables upon him.

Hattie: "The child never dreams!"

Félibien: "Never dreams!"

Hattie: "His own beauty suffices, I suppose. . . ."

Félibien: "Ah!"

Hattie: "I dream, of course, daytime, nighttime—*abundantly*. It is the secret of my youth." And Hattie describes her daydreams, her nighttime dreams, and her nightmares, which as far as Félibien can make out—for he is busy wondering why he has made the pretty little fellow angry—have to do with tea things —such as sugar-tongs, but always out of context:

"—and would you believe it! He had a pair of sugar-tongs *stuck in his ear!* And I said aloud—Why! Poor man! It's a *metronome!*"

"Who—who was that?" Félibien has been watching Amer pour the wine and break the bread against his breast.

"Beethoven! But, come to think of it, in my dream, although I *knew* it was Beethoven, he looked like Teddy Roosevelt! Anyway, I thought, *in my dream*, that is—Oh! So *that* explains why he's so blind, wretched thing—when I meant deaf of course. The tongs, thank God, weren't in his eyes! That would have been truly dreadful. . . .

29

"And I dreamt I was in the train, and there sitting opposite and wearing a seersucker suit was a gigantic pair of sugar-tongs! And I said to my husband who was sitting next to me, quite as alive as you and I—Why look! It's Beethoven! Only this time—now get this!—he looked like Bismarck! And then Amer came in with my cocoa and woke me up. Do you remember, Amer, darling? That dream I had?"

But Amer says nothing; his beautiful mouth the color of raw sea urchin is tightly shut.

"Bring in the dessert, dear boy." Hattie and Félibien watch Amer leave the room. "How ancient I have become!" Hattie cries, "and you both so young!" She pulls a wadded handkerchief out from between her breasts and blows her nose.

"My father used to say that all women over forty should be shot. Like horses, you know, for *glue!* Perhaps there is something to that—oh! *Come* now, Félibien. Whatever are you thinking of *now?* You're supposed to say, 'Of course not, Hattie! What a monster your father was! And you've outlived the old bastard by half a century already!' You know, it's strange," she continues, for she sees that she has caught his attention, "I dream of sugar-tongs and you stare at stains. What would Freud have said?"

"Frudd! The addict again. Who knows? You know I've never read him. Why should I? Priests, even defrocked priests, don't go in for hocus-pocus."

"Hocus-pocus he calls it! My arse, Félibien. You priests know nothing else. What was it you were saying just the other day about *delectationes morosas?* For Christ's sake! Oh! Forgive me, dear—I fear I'm a bit *tiddly.*"

Amer is back with an enormous floating island. Freshly made, it is still warm. And as he presents the dish to Félibien, he exhales the deliciously mingled odors of vanilla and fresh milk and caramel. Has he stolen a lick of the serving spoon? Little beggar! Little bugger! All at once Félibien is angry.

"Why don't you dream?" he asks Amer as he fills his dish with the stiff egg-whites and the unctuous yellow cream. "Everyone dreams!"

"Who knows what goes on in that handsome head?" Hattie

attempts to soothe him. Catching the fire in Amer's eyes, Félibien's heart kicks like an angry genie in a tightly sealed bottle. As for Hattie, she loves the boy's stubbornness; he reminds her of her youthful self.

Again he is gone.

"Coffee!" Hattie shouts after. And to Félibien: "He's only rude, you know, because you remind him of his brother."

"His brother!"

"But, darling. Surely you remember *that*—the little fellow who disappeared. Pfft! Out like a candle!"

"I can't recall."

"But he worked for you, dear, didn't he—before he ran away; or was *snatched away*," she laughs, sadly. "Poor boy's probably in a harem or—"

"Yes. I do seem to remember—but Amer has so many brothers and I—"

"Amer is ill at ease with you because he's superstitious. They are all so damned superstitious! Why—they are as bad as priests! Anyway, I'll send him away once we have our coffee, so you and I can talk without his incessant circling." When it comes, Hattie serves the coffee herself.

"He's a little witch," she continues after Amer is gone, "but gorgeous! Come—*confess*—I know you think he's gorgeous too! Why, look at you! As red as a candy apple! And you *can* confess you think he's cute. *I believe in love*," Hattie whispers. "I believe in love, Félibien, in *all* its shapes and sizes. . . . Darling! Are you on your way so soon?"

✴

Late afternoon . . . early evening. Félibien has been walking for hours. And now finds himself taking the path that leads to the gorge, the abyss that slides down and away from the roots of the domed and turreted city, a city of candy melting in the sun. He is followed by children—beggars! buggers!—but something tells them he is not to be meddled with. Tossing stones and insults in his direction, they scatter. Félibien is alone.

On the bridge that spans the gorge, Félibien falls to his knees.

His face and neck are still burning, and sting as if scratched and bitten. It is the fault of Amer, that black-eyed, sullen little beast, so like the other, the boy named Mouloud, his hireling, a shameless child with whom he had committed an undreamable act. But had he? Had the thing actually happened in the night shadows of the *bazar* when the floor becomes an ocean and he a captain and the child his first mate? Or second mate, or third mate. . . . How many times in blindness had he succumbed, seduced by lewd children! What would Frudd have said, and Hattie—had he confessed, *confessed to just what, exactly?* His brain is seething; it feels like it is building up steam. Any second a whistle will blow.

How confused he is. But the heat. For days and weeks after. For months after. The heat. And his mind bubbling like a bog. And he walking about, selling plastic pails, all the while encapsulated in hell.

How his flesh had tingled when the boy, Mouloud, held him; a boy of nettles, a boy of ardent coals. A sublime, a celestial boy. And Félibien is holding a creature of fire and venom in his arms, and the world smells of mint and money; yes, he gives Mouloud money, soft, finger-worn pieces, as soft as rabbit ears, the ears of pigs; and how soft the boy's testicles are, how extraordinarily thick and vigorous his prick, and he has seized it, hasn't he! It smokes between his lips.

Is this permitted? This promiscuity of thought? If only his memories, or fantasies, or whatever they are could be cut away from his brain and the wound cauterized. Either way he must confess. But not to Hattie! A priest is worse! He must confess it to himself.

Moaning, Félibien looks down at the famous hole in the ground, a hole in the world like a furry wound, and forces himself to be a mirror of his past, not to disregard or embellish anything; a cold, smooth mirror, heartless as ice, mindless as a knife, collecting particles of truth. He can see the impure atoms of his soul clinging to the mirror of his mind. His mirror is black and alive with terrifying shapes he dare not recognize.

As he sits on the bridge in an attitude of prayer, the mirror laps Félibien up. It is a thirsty mirror. First it drinks him down;

then it spits him out. And Félibien sees Félibien:

After dark. He sits alone in the *bazar*. The street door is locked. Has he locked Mouloud in without realizing it? Where has the little beast been hiding? If he has locked Mouloud in, it is because the boy wanted him to. The scum knows what he wants, knows what he is up to! The Devil's own excremental work is what the dirty boy Mouloud is up to!

After hours Félibien likes to dream. The ceiling is in bad repair and humidity has left peculiar traces, stains like bestial couplings and fields cluttered with the battered bodies of dead horses and their spilled intestines. But why must he think of such horrors? For it is true, his mind always wings back to horrors. His mind is a vulture winging back to a nest heaped with bloody lambs. His mind is a hungry wolf.

"I will fast! I will do penance, I—"

Félibien weeps; his face bathed in tears fills his hands. It is dusk. He is alone. Or is there a small, brown, beautifully hung boy crouching naked in the shadows?

Back in the *bazar* the room, and its shelves larded with rubber beach shoes and toys, is almost quiet. A rat gnaws at the cellophane wings of a mechanical moth. The moth circles once on the shelf with a small sound and, tumbling into the air, crashes. Its tiny, toothy gears and springs spill out like guts across the floor. There is a new smell in the endless night of the *bazar*, the sweet, peppery smell of sperm, the thicker smells of excrement and blood. But faint. As faint as the smell of well-buried death. Why should this be? Why is the fresh sawdust clotted with filth? Félibien sees this filth, he smells the blood, he sees himself sweeping. He sees the cellar trap. The chair put back over the trap, the chair where the merchant sits when he plays at captain. The feet of this familiar chair hammer on his heart.

"I am a pious man!" Félibien cries into the shadows that beak and talon him. But his voice is not Félibien's voice. It is the voice of a dog. A frightened dog, a pious dog—that most dangerous of dogs.

Clean

Dogs are dirty, birds are filthy, fish are clean except for the intestines which are dirty.

People love to wash and that's why in the eyes of Jesus they are best. Dogs don't go to Heaven, they turn into worms, but good Christian people stay just the same, younger and smelling good all the time. All the people get washed when they die and sit at the table of Holy Lightning with Jesus eating all that clean food. Jesus smiles when He sees the people washing. He knows that the people like to be clean and that's why He likes them better than the animals which eat any dirty crap.

Clean people who don't smell like vinegar sit at His table, only younger, with new hair, teeth, and skin, all naked but no fornicating, eating all that clean food. That's why it's important to get the old folks soaped and combed and into bed between sheets boiled four times and ironed into nice even creases— twelve creases for Jesus—and their toenails pared. Our old people look good, just simple folk, the color of milk and veal roast. When it's time Jesus calls them; He says: "Oh have you pared your nails?" And they answer: "Oh yes, sweet Lord, we have pared our nails and ironed our sheets twelve times." And Jesus says: "Are you *clean?*" Which is a joke because He knows they are and the old folks laugh a lot at this. And Jesus says: "Do you smell good and are you the color of roast veal?" And the old folks answer: "Oh yes, Lord, we are clean and our thoughts are like white sauce and our blood is like water and we are ready, oh sweet Jesus."

Then Jesus gathers them up in His arms and gives them clean teeth, the better to eat at His holy table, and clean ears, the better to hear His holy music, and clean eyes, the better to see and worship Him.

OUTER Spaces

She is tucked into herself, a letter addressed in invisible ink, sealed and inscrutable. Times she wails and batters pans (and all the pans are dented, and the clock is smashed, and the broom has lost its whiskers—what has he done?). Times she babies him, bakes gingerbread ladies and gentlemen; Boo sticks in the buttons and the eyes and eats them feet first. Times she just falls apart, huddles like a wet cuckoo tossled by the wind and nodding off. And Boo? He does what he can, his very best, and although he is only three, tries to foresee her moods. "Just fishing at ice holes for eels," his father would have told him. "Son, you're wasting your time."

But what are eels? But what are holes of ice?

Boo clasps his own hands. He has little else to hold. Time rolls past as gracelessly as his own sticky alphabets.

❋

Boo jumps when she suddenly unsnaps—who's turned the key at the small of her back?

"Well! Boo! Look who!" she starts from her trance shrilly piping. "Noah? Waiting on the whale? Waiting as dolphins claim the vineyards and the woods? Noah! And I didn't *know it!*"

Boo bubbles over, laughing his head off, pleased as peaches when this peculiar bird-woman, his mother, this whale of a mystery is back. Back from where? Back to earth, his father might have said, back home to Boo—with an inscrutable joke (What's a vineyard? What's a dolphin?) and a fairy story, maybe a riddle cupped in her hands. She raises them now to his face, as if secreting something very precious: a griffin's egg, a ruby ring, a castle key. And if she often forgets to feed him, Boo rarely goes to bed without a story.

"Once there was a moon inhabited by birds; they spoke in human words and made their nests in thorns and burrs, and for kisses pecked at one another's bills; they collected string, they dove for pearls, they manufactured mattresses of bread-crumbs. . . ."

She speaks quickly, vividly, before falling into incoherence:

"Pickle, tickle, snakes in the boots—"

Boo's father has no patience whatsoever with what he calls her "fucking outer spaces"; Boo and his mother live alone.

✳

She cuts out targets for his marbles: twelve Tweedledums and Tweedledees of shoe-box cardboard with silver-paper swords, and puts a dish of milk down in the corner for the fairy he has never seen, when all at once she is weeping. His father would have whispered: "She's gone fruity, son, ba-na-nas. Pay her no mind."

Tweedle, tweedle, tweedle. She's been twiddling her thumbs all afternoon. Some madwomen knit the air, some squash imaginary wasps between their forefingers and their thumbs. Boo is five. If he thinks to ask her and if she cares to answer, surely she replies:

"Doing? Twiddling."

Bored to tears, Boo scrabbles around, finds a box of crackers, and takes them to bed with the bear he calls Boom-Boom.

✳

She is terrified of the Outside. Groceries are delivered by the man she calls Nervous Mervish. Despite the soot that tumbles from the sky, she grows giant toadstools and dwarfs in a garden the size of a closet. There is a birdbath that he and Boom-Boom can see from his bedroom window. With wings like rainbows the birds scatter the water. Droplets are diamonds hanging in the air.

If the Outside tempts him, he has inherited her panic. How could it be otherwise? He watches the unwholesome world from his window.

Dad never comes except to scold them both, to violate their intimacy and shatter their fragile peace. When he leaves it is worse than ever; times she hasn't the energy to twiddle her thumbs or bake an apple. Nights the sounds of sirens opacify their dreams. The subway sets her teeth to rattling when she tells her stories:

"Beneath murmuring waters, a girl was born with a coiling tail. Squids sang to her, sluggish shellfish clustered at her throat. She breathed spray, Boo, and she wept a lot. Her name was . . . Dew. Sopping Dew. And she was . . . appointed. Appointed by Sir Hygrometer himself. Her Highness of Humidity. And she lived in Mindless Torpor."

✳

Boo is six. When the pumpkin yellow schoolbus comes for him, his fear is so great he falls to the path with a thud like a troll's iron hammer. Petrified, Boo and Boom-Boom spend the next few weeks watching the bus smear past the window. Yet Boo cannot help but wonder about the small faces he sees pressed like grapefruit against the glass. And then one night, he dreams he drives the bus himself.

She tells him a story about a chuckle-headed boy who drives a bus into the sun and sets the world on fire. All that is left of the world is a chunk of coal and all that is left of the boy is a hank of charred hair. The smell of burning is teeming on the air. She has burned his porridge.

"I-if I was the b-b-bus d-d-driver, I-I c-could t-take you f-for rides!" Boo stutters because he knows he is being stubborn.

The dream coincides with the visit of the mysterious, honey-colored Miss Dionesia. One day the doorbell rings and there she is, smiling at Boo with what strikes him as genuine sweetness.

"We would all like you so very much to come to school, Boo!" She squeezes two of his fingers in a friendly, teasing manner he enjoys. He wishes that just this once his mother would come out of the closet.

"M-m-may Boo-Boom-Boom come too?" The gingerbread

person is down on her knees, toying with the one button that has not yet fallen from Boo's tattered shirt. He knows that his mother, barely breathing, is in the hall closet, listening.

"Of course you can bring Boom-Boom." She strokes the bear's belly gently with her hand. "There are several bears in school."

When she leaves, his mother comes out into the hall looking battered. Boo feels his heart tear in two. But he knows that he and Boom-Boom are about to embark on a great adventure.

That afternoon he sits on the front stoop. When the schoolbus passes, he sees the children's faces clearly. They are as magical as exotic fish hovering in a clean tank.

"Did you *see*, Boom-Boom?"

＊

Boo asks his mother to buy him a lunch box; nobody else takes sandwiches to school wrapped in newspaper. He will never know the monumental effort it takes her to walk all the way to the department store. He will never tell her that the pink box with Snow White stenciled on the lid was intended for a little girl. He trades it for another and tells her that his own has been stolen, that the dented, rusty tin he brings home is a gift.

The thought of the theft ferrets away at her heart and keeps her from sleeping. And she fears the rusty box with the masked man on its lid may poison her son's lunches. She stains cream cheese green with vegetable coloring. When in the early morning he skips up the path to the bus, he no longer sees her startled eyes. He has forgotten to kiss her. He has left Boom-Boom behind.

Boo's request for peanut butter causes her to crumple and slam shut like the jack-in-the-box he plays with at school.

"Peanut butter?" she gasps, surfacing at last. "From what sort of udder, Boo, comes this other butter?" He is the only boy in school with blue peanut butter sandwiches. He finds he can trade these for anything he wants, even homemade cherry pie.

＊

Evenings he comes home to the sun-speckled, ratty yard with her things—painted plaster frogs and peeling windmills, old tires filled with pebbles from the sea, and fishbowl deep-sea divers; tiny pagodas that glow in the dark. These things have excited his friends' curiosity. Boo wants to bring them home after school. She looks at him in disbelief when he tells her both boys are named George.

"Th-they want t-to see the dwarfs up c-close!" he explains. He sees that he has startled her. "Th-they w-want to play with th-the little bridges. Th-they won't b-b-b-break anything, M-ma—" he adds hopefully. "They ain't r-rough."

She is cooking rice and in the silence he can hear it sticking to the bottom of the pan. What is she thinking of? Her hands jiggle between her knees.

"YOU COULD BE FAIRY COBBLERS!" She jumps up from her chair and, knocking it over, runs to the closet and pulls out three pairs of high-heeled party shoes he has never seen her wear.

☀

As the wheels of the schoolbus spin past, so passes time: seven, eight, nine. He feels guilty when his paper route brings him home late, and years later, when he leaves town for business school, guiltier still.

He comes home for weekends. She prepares festive stews of her own invention: at the last minute she adds candied cherries, or parsley cut from magazines. Once she serves him an entire magazine meal: roast chicken, glazed carrots, and chocolate cake.

He no longer asks what she does with her time. He knows she spends her life folded into herself, visiting a garden he can no longer imagine, her secret cities, his father might have said, of Gog and Magog. When once he shows up unexpectedly with a Chinese omelette, she startles him when she says:

"Hennig's left foot, stocking and all, grew up out of his grave, you know, like a mushroom! Looked like a mushroom! Folks took it to *be* a mushroom! This room's a mess!" she adds, the first lucid thing he has heard her say in years.

39

Once he brings a girl with him. Superbly agitated, his mother spends the entire week making canapés. When they arrive the yard is littered with stale crusts. Fat squirrels scold them from the roof. Inside the house, marshmallows are stuck to foam igloos in all the rooms. He holds his breath and bravely asks:

"Mother! Well! And what have you been doing?"

"Ding? Dong?" she answers. As if to shield herself from wild animals, she crouches behind a chair, exalted and sneezing. The girl, whom Boo adores, suppresses a giggle and shivers, from nerves or the cold, he cannot say. When they leave his mother mortifies him by shouting:

"Peek a Boo!"

He is furious with the girl when, in the bus on the way home, she collapses with laughter.

✳

Twenty, thirty, forty. Like the birds, time flies.

Boo is middle-aged and broken and mended so often he likes to joke bitterly to his friends that his joints are all made of rubber cement. These days he is always sad, and—even in his wife's embrace—lonely.

Late in the winter Boo receives a telephone call from a hospital. His mother has been found wandering barefoot in the snow. He drives for seven hours through the thickening, freezing air to a city he does not recognize. He is surprised by the hospital's size. Ghostlike figures gravitate in the half-light of the halls and each open door is a doorway to Hell.

Her room, when he finds it, is very large. Tubes and wires prod the ceiling like forked hazel wands. She is lying on her back. Her hair is chalky white. To her left a large woman sits immodestly, knitting air. To her right a beautiful stranger crushes invisible insects between her fingers. His mother's hands are cupped together. He longs to see what it is she is hiding: a gem? an egg? a castle key?

As Boo bends over the bed to look into her clotted eyes, her thin, frostbitten nose pecks away at the strangeness hanging between them like a transparent pane of glass.

40

Electric Rose

ELECTRIC ROSE. See her dipping down the garden path, her beak thrust nervously forward: one step to the left, three to the right, a fluttering of wings, then, hastily, she gobs a mouthful of petals, juicy, sour-sweet. Chews abstractedly. Swallows and crows. And remembers with a grin that once someone called her his *pussycat*.

UNWIND! Her flesh a solid block of blue-veined gneiss. They took her away fossilized, her eyes tacked to the upholstery. She stayed that way two days. They hacked away, hacked away, broke her into bite-size pieces, forced her throat open to receive

LIFE. She spoke to her heart, held the lid tight shut, wanting to sleep so much. They strapped her to a chair and showed her color slides of her father hanging by his neck in the kitchen (she recognized the linoleum); her baby clasped by the small, white coffin; the kitchen again, the smashed stove: *Does she remember anything?*

YES. Her face wet, they said: *She is snapping out of it*. And plugged her in. They watched her lurch and go limp; before their eyes she was metamorphosed into a pool of mucus. They nodded and said: *We have brought her back*. And went out for a cup of coffee.

FOR CENTURIES SHE LAY THERE in a blue cup, camphor packed in her skull and sex. She was full of loathing. She longed for bones clean of meat. For the purity of ashes.

There was always a light above me. For a time I thought it was God. Then I saw it was just an ordinary light bulb and I laughed.

Brillig

When the poison had come in the form of treason as fore-
seen in the prognostications of the Perfect, the Jumblies,
having survived sabotage and a punitive somersault through
alien space, founded Outpost Number One upon the only hab-
itable island of the Thousand-Thousand—those extravagant
regions that could never be mapped.

The Thousand-Thousand fluctuate in a perpetual state of
inexplicable process. A clement sky will oscillate like the lid of
a coffin, sealing everything in darkness no fire can lighten, nor
reverie illuminate. In that vertiginous obscurity the planet's ge-
ography scrambles. The star is notoriously inhospitable; its living organisms decline and extinguish with hair-raising celerity.

The Jumblies tarried by no choice of their own. Thrust into
Brillig's chastening orbits, their ship unassociated into spectral
leaks and crashed. Sustained by bitter roots and the bile of exile, the Jumblies fought the fingers of ferns and, prying entry
into those wastes of evasive voices, claimed the husks they
needed to construct Outpost Number One.

The outpost was built in what the Jumblies named Sector
Seventy-Seven of the Thousand-Thousand. But because sectors
burglarize from one another, all definitions are tenuous. The
outpost periodically loses members and parts. These material-
ize elsewhere. An example among many: one of the Jumblies
claimed to have seen in a perplexing region of fleece and tar
the smile of a former mistress abducted (he swore to it) by fog.

According to oral tradition, hard edges were perceived for
the first time during an instantaneous drought. Horizons took
on the comforting definitions of flagstaffs and steeples. Once
these had been invested with the powerful names of the Old
Gods, those unutterable names that give permanency and pro-
tection, they vanished. It was then that the Perfect argued with

the greatest conviction that all things are illusory, especially when, tall and sharp, they would mock Heaven. He made a solemn joke of it—something to do with jesting and jousting—but his exact words have been mangled by the mouths of the many.

The drought transformed Brillig into a tangle of combustible trash the Jumblies feared would ignite in the heat of starlight, ending their miserable sojourn in conflagration. Instead, chameleons materialized in the rubbish with outsized eyes that spun in their heads like wheels. They could not be eaten, nor could the future be retrieved from their bowels—as they had none. They brought to mind an ancient narrative—something to do with flintboxes and enchantment. To punish himself for not having had the perspicacity to commit this tale to memory, the Perfect, swearing by the purity of his inner vehicles, mortified his testicles with thorns.

It was in this parched season that the Jumblies dragged forth the first Eggs. The Perfect warned that the Egg was taboo as the unborn, unblemished by Time, are sacred. The more heretical insisted that the gift of Eggs proved that Fate was looking after them still and that rather than quibble, the Perfect should himself partake of the feast. He refused and was left to jabber on his mat. Not long after he was found dead, his throat slit from ear to ear in the ceremonial manner.

That night the Jumblies tied themselves to trees for fear of being swept to deadlier zones. They watched in impotent horror as the Eggs gave day to dragons with the faces of owls. But if monsters tormented the Jumblies as they hung from trees like puppets from posts, they endured this affliction as they had others before, and after celebrated future victories in frantic fornications—celebrations smartly squelched by a sudden rain of volcanic ash.

Deep in their heart of hearts the Jumblies wondered why Gods once generous had now chosen to torture them. Was this the price of spacegreed? Would they never again know Order and Plenitude—ideals they had worshiped on aching knees in the pronged temples of their lost world? Their dreams were troubled by visions of demons with hooks who toyed with their bodies as idle children afflict frogs with mirrors and wire.

43

Briefly I will describe the Jumblies: their heads are green and their hands are blue; they are naked and bad-tempered; their babies are born blemished by a shocking growth of black hair recalling the tufted epaulettes of senescent subtropical terrestrial baboons. Some Jumblies have tails. We may have seen snouts. They are all short, they snort, they dribble, they argue nonsense, they venerate spotted beans; above all they goggle alarmingly at visitors. These brutes are no more vessels of Light, but cages of Night bolted shut by the savage demands of this, the darkest of planets.

✳

The Jumblies have come to cherish their harrowing existence. They could not tell us how long they have been marooned; each and every one of them hotly insists he is the descendant of an extinct species of shellfish. Had their stunted memories been sharper, still they could not have told us much: time is figured loosely in epochs named for the planet's shiftless moods and the evil spells of its seasons.

Of their starship nothing remains. Mud-colored jellyfish vegetate in the ooze where she crashed; only glass has withstood that swindle called a climate. The Jumblies have used her established orderings of copper to coronate their Perfect, yet say the crown is the gift of Figurant Archons from a drug-induced dream. The Jumblies dream abundantly and from that other nebulous star have brought back the many squalid practices that typify Brilligeois culture—including a method for keeping the cult Eggs intact by soaking them in quicksand boiled in urine. To each his owl-faced dragon; the Jumblies choose to preserve, hatch, else smash his own—unhatched—to bits, at puberty.

The Jumblies looked upon us with hostility. When the questionable surface upon which we had teleported began to fumble with our cellular interpreters (and some feared with our minds), we departed.

The Jumblies and their Perfect could not know that we were responsible for the seeding of Brillig with their precarious lives,

44

and yet, as we rose in a puff of smoke, they turned their scowling faces to the sky and shook their fists. Knowing nothing of gravity, one went so far as to throw a rock. It fell back and knocked out most of his teeth.

We abandoned the abject formlessness of Brillig in time to see a wall of muck sweep across the overhang upon which we had stood instants before cringing in the gloom. A skeptic among us has been converted to the Faith; the visit to Brillig has convinced him that the entire physical universe is an invention of demons.

Missy

"Die, Little Mae!"
       Missy is sitting in the front of the schoolbus and she says this just as Little Mae steps off. Startled, Little Mae turns her head and stares back into Missy's pale blue eyes. Are there holes in Missy's head? Little Mae sees the sky shining right through!

"Bye!" Missy says brightly. "Bye! Little Mae!"

＊

Missy is in her bath. She is an ugly little girl. Her face is much too long, her body uncannily long, as if made of rubber she had been pulled from her mother's womb and stretched. Rubber is Missy's emblem: in the bouncing ball see the Cosmic Dance!

＊

The head crowns and the doctor has not yet arrived. Grandmother pushes with both palms against the baby's skull, keeping it tied up in limbo for over thirteen minutes. When the doctor comes and lets the baby out, she comes out long.

"The limbs on her!" curses Grandmother. "Poor little spider-child!"

＊

Today Missy is nine and the universe is pink. The hot bubble bath popping at her navel, her skin in the hot water, the birthday dress, ironed and fluffed out and waiting on the bed, her bed, its sheets and covers and the foamy carpeting.

Dogs, monkeys, rabbits, and birds are crowded together on

Missy's bed. She sleeps with them. All night long their obsidian eyes watch over the lethal flower of her body. They can see everything and they are eaters: eaters of ghosts, ghouls, and witches. They watch over Missy, and Missy watches over them. When the sun rises she counts to be certain that no one has been left behind during the shivering passage through the night.

❋

After the bath, Mother rouges Missy's cheeks. Missy admits that she looks "prettier" this way, but she is not pleased. She knows that it is her pale white skin, white as an egg, that, stretched tightly across her impassive face, is so impressive. Now that she is out of her bath, dried and dressed, her paleness has returned—as has a persistent chill in her hands and feet. Her ears are always unaccountably cold as well.

"Egg!" Granny had said. "Egg! Why so cold? Shall we put some pepper on to hot her up? Eh? Pepper pot?" and she had nibbled Missy's ear. But that was long ago, so long ago! Granny had been the only one to dare take such liberties with Missy.

❋

"It is my birthday and I am nine," Missy says solemnly to the animals all lined up according to species and size along the floor.

"We are the same age, well nearly, darling Wool!" she says to an aged cotton lamb who has lost its eyes and most of its fluff. "And you must all work very hard for me today, all of you!" she continues, her hands clasped tightly across her heart. "Little Mae will be here," she adds in a whisper, "and you all know how much we all hate Little Mae! Here! Goosey! You'll be Little Mae—but just for today, poor darling, and I'll make it up to you later, I promise!"

Goosey is placed in the center of the floor—a small, brown rabbitish thing covered with the tiny bumps that gave him his name; the others are placed around him.

"Now! Watch Goosey and think about Little Mae! Think the most terrible things you can, terrible, *horrible things!*"

47

＊

"Hi! Little Mae!"

＊

The doorbell begins to ring; it will ring intermittently for the next thirteen minutes—Missy's guests are punctual. There are nine of them. Ill at ease in Missy's expensive house they perch at the edge of the gold-upholstered furniture and whisper nervously together until Missy arrives, taking everything in hand and leading them all out to the back lawn.

Pink orchids in ornate vases stand in each corner of the stone terrace, and the picnic table—hidden beneath a glossy embroidered cloth—is decorated with garlands of popcorn and an ornate arrangement of flesh-colored peaches. The linen is white and the gold-banded porcelain dishes dazzle like nine solar disks. Each guest's name is tucked into her napkin along with an orchid: PRISSY MELBA LOLLY LORETTA LITTLE MAE TINA SALLY-ANN FANNY and—at the head of the table—MISSY. The presents (invitations had specified: *gifts will be pink*) have been stacked by Missy's dish; she has them removed and placed in the house. Missy feels that opening gifts in public is in very bad taste.

Missy sits stiffly, regally; the rouge and her unusual size give her the aura of a grown-up. The others cannot help but admire her and feel proud that they belong to this magic inner circle. Little Mae also sits very still; she is waiting for the hatchet to fall, but it doesn't, not yet. It stays in midair, just above Little Mae's braided head. Missy is even smiling at her. But such a *cold* smile!

＊

"She hates me, Mother!" sobs Little Mae. But Mother insists: "Now, Little Mae! She can't hate you! She wouldn't have invited you! It just makes no sense!"

Little Mae is thinking: *It makes no sense!* And she clasps the gorgeous linen napkin that flows across her lap and claws at it mindlessly with her little polished nails.

The cake arrives. It is a great frosted nine-story temple decorated with candy corn and marzipan babies. Missy dismisses the maid and cuts the big pink and white slices herself, being careful to give each guest one baby. Little Mae sees that her baby has no head and bites her lip. The maid returns with a green dish of raspberry ice cream.

Missy lifts her fork and the girls eat; they arch their pinkies and *ooh!* and *ahh!* like great ladies; the cake is *heavenly, heavenly! It is like a cloud, light as a feather! Really, Missy, it is made of wind!*

Missy tells them that it was baked especi.lly for her birthday and that it came early that morning in a sparkling white truck—

"Like an ambulance," she adds, turning her eyes upon Little Mae, "only very much bigger."

Little Mae cannot bear Missy's eyes and tearfully stares into her dish. She is a sickly child—obviously not tough enough to belong to the select group of Missy's friends. But then why was she invited? The others all look at Little Mae curiously. . . .

✳

Missy is talking about Mexico. Her uncle lives there.

"What's he live in *Mexico* for?" asks the astonished Prissy, certain that the only civilized place to live is Georgia.

"There's *oil* in Mexico, silly!" says Missy. "And temples and great pyramids. The Aztecs built them."

"*Ass-peckers!*" Loretta gasps and the girls all laugh—even Missy laughs and so they all laugh freely, gleefully until the tears stream from their eyes. It is the party's first good laugh and everyone is grateful to Loretta. Little Mae manages to jam some pink slush into her mouth and to swallow.

"Aztecs!" Missy shouts very suddenly and somewhat sternly. And all the girls fall silent. "Aztecs," says Missy softly. "They used to cut off people's heads."

"*Their heads!*" the girls, wonderfully scandalized, all gasp together.

"They cut them off and strung them on sticks—like pearls," Missy continues; and catching Little Mae with her eyes: "But first they cut out their hearts!"

And suddenly Little Mae is sick, seized and shaken in the spiked fist of a fit; foam fills her mouth and her body arches backwards; she falls to the floor with a loud thud and lies there, rigid, as if tied and knotted inside an invisible sack. And as the girls all scream and scatter, the maid comes and gently lifts Little Mae in her strong black arms. Cradling her to her bosom, she carries her far from that terrible place.

❋

The sun has set. The party is over and Missy has gone to her room to sleep. Goosey is still in the middle of the floor surrounded by the others.

"Poor, poor Goosey!" Missy cries, picking him up in her arms. "But you were marvels, simply marvels, all of you!" she cries. "Little Mae was so sick! So sick! And I am so proud of you! But now," she wonders as she places the animals all back on her bed in readiness for sleep, "what shall we do with Goosey? He's poisoned! Poisoned to the core! Poor Goosey! He'll have to be killed, he'll have to die, and he'll have to die tonight! He can't stay with us any longer—you do all see that, don't you?"

And as everyone agrees, Goosey is taken to the bathroom and quartered with a pair of very sharp scissors, his stuffing spilled into Missy's private toilet.

"Nothing remains of Goosey!" Missy cries gaily to the others. "All the bad has been flushed away!" And then, with childlike glee so unlike herself, Missy takes a running leap and jumps into bed.

The Star Chamber

At dusk he was brought before the Star Chamber. We stripped him of his clothes; we cut his belly open so that he could hide nothing. We taped up his mouth and asked him to speak. He would not answer our questions although we beat him repeatedly about the face and feet.

At dawn we kneaded him into a loaf and charred him in our vast ovens of fire. Later we broke this loaf and fed it to the poor.

Now in the streets they whisper that the loaf could not be eaten. And a strange new hunger that cannot be silenced spreads across the land.

The Tale of the Tattooed Woman

Mutilation has enhanced my beauty, and if this were an age when men worshiped marvels, they would bring more than thin coins to see me. They would bring the rarest things they own. They would give what I would ask. I would ask for particles of flesh.

But I am not complaining. These days who gives a damn for Bearded Lady? Who languishes for Lizard Girl? Their threadbare tents are empty. Yet men crush to see me and line up for tickets like ants tracking sugar. Many leave with broken hearts. They return again and again to tell me I am opium, the beautiful vampire who bleeds their nights of sleep. Some speak of love, but I know better. It is my surface they love, that fantastic snare. If they saw me as you do, they would hide their tails and run.

For I am hateful. You see that. You have never been taken in, not even for a moment, and from the first perceived the truth.

Years ago you asked me how it began. You have been patient, and strangely enough, unafraid. This has endeared you to me. Fearlessness should be rewarded. Today I will tell you my story. But quickly. Words are treacherous. I have always preferred silences.

I was born a twin. The effort killed my mother. And the other, a bloated, lopsided thing, also died. I took a breath and screamed. I screamed for seven years.

I was never still. When toads or scarabs fell into my hands I tore them to shreds and looked on laughing when ants carried the gritty droplets of ordure to their clotted cellars. Everything angered me. My dolls, their waxy faces and china hands, my bland picture books and animals of ivory. My father gave me a canary. In a tantrum I bit off its head. Despairing, he threatened to lock me away forever so that this world of creatures and things would be safe.

For a time I carried my hatred sheathed like a dagger within me. Life was peaceful. Roses grew in the garden. I consumed my rice and milk and no longer trampled my dresses to shreds. I forced myself to contemplate the gutless images in my glossy books and nursed a swollen doll with a fat and foolish face. I took naps. I was good. So good that for Christmas my father gave me that greatest of gifts—trust—in the shape of a flat-nosed pug of such high race it could barely breathe. I liked to watch it tear meat apart with its odd little mismatched teeth. A stupid animal, it loved me dearly. It slept at the foot of my bed. For hours each night I caressed its thick neck, feeling the life throb there. Then one day I coaxed it into a trap that the gardener had set for a vixen. I watched it bleed to death. The beast's agony flooded my heart with delight.

Fear came after. And the terrible knowledge that my appetite for destruction was insatiable. With a pen from my father's study and stolen ink, I pressed a mark beneath my skin, a blue tattoo on my wrist to remind me *never to kill again.*

And here it is, a black seed lost in a forest, the molecular center of a diminutive rose. And the rose is one blossom in a garland of blossoms, leaves, and purple thorns that circle my wrist, very like those at my ankles and throat.

It is time for you to go. Outside the public is stirring impatiently. Soon my satin cape will fall to the floor with a hiss. You have said that my garlands, mere decorations, cannot compare in beauty to those black horses doing battle upon my breasts and the red dragon whose blinded eye is my navel; the wounded eagle you once especially admired and the centaurs wrestling to the death upon my thighs. My forest fires, my sensuous nudes, my feral tigers have not faded.

Max, Moleskin, and Glass

A century ago the authoress Maxine Taffin Pérou was immensely popular. Today she is ignored. She wrote over thirty novels now consigned to oblivion. D'Arcy Lapoisse buried what was left of her fading reputation when he likened her style to "certain funebrial gardens with far too many raked gravel paths leading absolutely nowhere."

Maxine's contracts required that each volume be bound in moleskin. Each featured a recent photograph. There is a startling portrait of Max wearing nothing but a necklace of boiled lobsters. It is the very photograph André Breton describes as having had a disruptive influence upon the collective imagination of lunatics at the turn of the century. It is more than likely, it is certain, that her monstrous success, and there was something monstrous about her success, had little to do with literature and much to do with her boyish beauty, that lobster necklace, her fierce affairs with chambermaids, and the persistent rumors of her death. Yet after she had perished diving into the sea after naked statuary, or leaping from a silk balloon, Max would be seen fit as a fiddle stepping out with her splendid secretary, a murderously strapping Scotsman, or in a box at the opera loudly laughing.

Each novel offers a portrait: Max petulant in tassels, Max clowning at the beach, Max vamping beneath a fantastical turban. And when crows left their tracks at the corners of her eyes, the house photographer placed a piece of gauze over the lens. She could have done without it. To the very last Max was a stunning, wide-eyed anorexic with endearing shoulder blades.

Max's publishers did well by her and came to accept any eccentric demand she made. Her contracts specified that she was to receive seven dozen oysters a week. At death she was to be fitted out by the celebrated taxidermist St. Hilaire and kept in her apartment beneath a glass bell. When at the age of seventy-four her heart failed her, the thing was done and her remains—or whatever one wishes to call them—stuffed with horsehair and prodded into a pair of taffeta pajamas, were wedged into a chair beside the writer's small Byzantine desk. One hand was sewn to her temple in a reflective attitude, and the other wired to a pen poised above the celebrated sentence she never finished:

"The drum major's lashes hovered over eyes so dark that they might have been pools of purple ink, although they were in fact black, but this the Minister of the Interior was soon to find out although not—"

❋

The fragmented *Drum Major* was published posthumously. A pernickety editor pointed out that Max's contract called for a photograph of her corpse. The photographer was dispatched at once and introduced into her apartments by the secretary. He was relieved to observe that despite everything, and against all expectations, Max looked nearly alive. With unanticipated skills, St. Hilaire had tightened skin, inserted teeth, and removed a growth that had developed beneath the novelist's nose in later years. Her great glass eyes appeared to dream. Those famous shoulder blades sallied as she dipped over the unfinished sentence. The book enjoyed tremendous success and all winter long bookstalls reverberated with the enthusiastic detonations of collectors of the macabre.

A year or so later *The Doorpost and the Herring* was due for reprinting. This time Max appears in profile and the effectiveness of this particular portrait resides in a nearly imperceptible shift of one of her glass eyes. Her beauty seemed eternal. Her publishers feared the public would lose interest in these static poses. Max had been sewn into her chair. But nothing is eternal, not even an expertly tanned hide kept under glass. In the dry clime of the Sahara Max's mummy might have done better. But this is Paris, the winters are damp, the apartment is encumbered with African violets and the Scotsman partial to bubble

55

and squeak. Vapors collect inside the bell.

One terrible day the photographer receives an urgent message. The writer's wrist has snapped. With pitiful insistence the disembodied hand remains stuck to the cadaver's rouged cheeks. The photographer takes pictures. The man is a rogue and he sells these to necrophiliacs. The secretary takes a cut. St. Hilaire tidies things up with paraffin and string. But the word gets out and soon only melancholics buy Max's books. Even her fans cannot look at the moleskin volumes without sickening. Many stop reading altogether.

The collapse of Max's bosom coincides with the end of her lease. The police get wind of the affair and insist on a proper burial. With commendable if latent pudicity, a scatologically inclined nephew appears to remove the body and bell. Badly foxed and matted in a Marie-Louise so purple it appears to be black, the unfinished sentence can still be seen hanging in one of the publisher's unfrequented antechambers.

Jungle

Walter loved Leila Maleysh madly. You laugh. You say, "What? Walter Bongo? That pip-squeak?" Yet it is true. Walter loved her madly, and she, of course, despised him. Right from the start she told the *gefiyeh* that his ears were too big, that his skull was too flat, that his feet and hands were no bigger than a monkey's. What she did not tell him was worse: that his pants rumpled in the seat because he had no arse to speak of, and what good is a man without an arse? She hated the swamp green suit he wore when he went to see her, and she hated Walter's gifts of baklava that he bought from the leper— why didn't he know any better? What she wanted was a real man with a big arse and big hands who would bring her European whiskey in fancy foil wrappers.

He never knew this. He didn't understand her. He worshiped her breasts, which were very full and round, with hard, fat nipples pointing down to the tiled floor from some freakish tropism. He admired these breasts and dreamt lovingly of grasping them and nestling in her lap like a little baby, or a monkey to suckle there sweetly. He dreamt of this and nothing more and because, God knows, it was not enough, she detested him. And she humiliated him!

One night Walter went to Leila wearing his green suit and a new tie clip in the form of a crocodile. When he knocked shyly at her door, clutching the little oily bag of baklava for dear life, she saw the crocodile at once. Even before he had taken off his fez she said, "Is it gold?" And Walter, dismayed because he thought she was referring to a new false tooth said, "Yes. I am sorry." Leila insisted, "No it isn't. Give it to me and I'll show you." She took it off very slowly, all the while pressing against Walter. She noticed that he was blushing and this made her even more vicious than usual. He followed her to the kitchen where she took a bowl from a shelf and filled it with bleach. "No, please, Leila . . ." he whined. "What are you going to do? *What are you doing?*" Walter watched sadly as the crocodile changed from gold to grey to green. I believe he may have wept. In a moment its two little red eyes fell out. "It matches your jungle suit now," Leila said, and for some reason she felt tender. That evening Leila Maleysh let Walter Bongo into her bed, but first she set a number of obstacles before him. She was surprised to find that without his suit he was a man like any other and really not too bad-looking. In the fray the crocodile was lost. She found it under the bed months later, stuck to the floor.

ThRIƒT

The chosen infants are taken from their mothers after the sixth week. They are placed in specialized hospitals and tortured. Other than that they are treated like other children; washed, hushed, scolded, and kissed.

They are tortured every day at varying intervals for their entire lives. Within a few years they are all fancifully deformed. None live long, the oldest die broken and senile and sixteen.

They never reach puberty or grow taller than four feet. However, individual members (hands, fingers, tongues, feet, and ears) develop and grow to miraculous lengths.

When these children die they are fed to the police dogs.

Nothing on the planet is ever wasted.

Bedtime Story

When the wolves came to that country
They pulled up the bridges
When the lice came to that country
They burned the houses and
When the crabs came to that country
They rolled up the rivers and threw them away
When the snakes came to that country
They broke all the trees and burned the forests
When the sharks came to that country
They turned the seas to vapor
When the vultures came to that country
They flooded the deserts and they closed the skies
When the lions came to that country
They leveled the mountains
They leveled the mountains and flattened the hills
When the lizards came they filled the hollows with sand
And when the armies of men came to that country
Nothing was left to be done
And they rejoiced

The Monkey Lover
An Authentic Tale from Baklava

My husband, that ridiculous worm, had an upside-down head, being profusely bearded and totally bald. As he slept I liked to imagine that the red beard was a wig, the bare dome a chin, and the open mouth, so terrible in slumber, a pistol wound in the forehead. Had he been a better man, such thoughts may never have entered my head. But as things were, these visions tormented me until there was no peace for either of us. The man was a pig, his chin inscribed with nasty scrawls of nicotine, mustard, and chocolate: for his mouth was forever full of things dark and viscous, as was his brain. And although young enough to be his daughter, if I had ceased to laugh whenever I chanced to see myself reflected in the glass or catch a glimpse of a toad lurching across the porch in the moonlight, it was because my laughter excited him and my smiles made him gloat with pleasure. He thought then that I was happy. . . .

"Are you happy, Saida, my little fishcake?" he would dribble, taking my ears in his paws and pretending to box them. "Are you happy, my little blue fig?" grabbing my childish breasts in his terrible paws that smelled of a goat's testicles. "Come sit on my knees and play the tongue game with your papa."

His name was Dung Baba. Promoted by Fate to Chief of Police, he loved his job, which provided the flesh he toyed with as a sow toys with a walnut, rolling it back and forth through the dust with her snout until all at once exasperated she smashes the shell and swallows the meat with one noisy gulp.

My husband's savagery was notorious. Persons who had been caught sleeping under the bridge or secreting chick peas in their pockets were brought to him twitching like worms in puddles of mud. He trussed them to oddly stained poles. He humiliated and maimed them in a thousand unexpected ways.

Of these truths I knew little, swaddled as I was in my child-bride shifts and fear of the monster, the web of my father's lies and my mother's resigned mutterings. In Baklava a girl must take what Allah tosses her way with a scraping and a bowing and a blinking down at her feet.

It is said that Allah owns a filing cabinet. Sealed with the blood of the hymen, all marriage contracts are kept therein. When with a smart clap of thunder the drawer is slammed shut, nothing can open it, not even death. A widow, no matter how young, must never again look upon a man, be he her own brother. Locked in the kitchen, she is forbidden everything: visits, speech, self-love; forbidden to pass the milk and dates through the little window in the wall no bigger than a brick lying on its side.

I called Dung Baba's house the cage; in his kitchen my dreams decayed. The house was circumscribed by a high wall of earth and date pits; rooting in the earth the pits had formed an impenetrable barrier. As is the custom, I picked stones from the lentils and scraped the dung from my master's boots which were set out for my attention, nightly. If at dawn the boots were imperfect in any way, Dung Baba invented a punishment. Such was my life.

I was lonely, childless. I pleaded with Dung Baba for a little monkey to play with, but he refused angrily, grumbling that animals were as detestable to him as men. Next I prayed to Allah whose ears are deaf; then did I beseech his fallen twin, the devil Hornprick, who upon his throne of fire gloats upon his constellations and counts his bloody seeds.

In Baklava it is said that Hornprick once caught a glimpse of the First Woman as she sat singing to her snake in her chamber of sacred mud. Dazzled by her sight, the light of love and lust, he fell. He is still falling. For all eternity her breasts orbit his dreams.

Hornprick listened to me. Without delay, he sent me little Kishkishkat the monkey. At dawn he leapt over the wall. I was breathless with the wonder of his small beauty. My furry grasshopper! Even his voice was small. It was easy to coax him to eat dates from my lips and soon he let me fondle and caress him. I knew love and laughter. In time I gave birth to a beautiful daughter.

Naatiffe was covered in soft pink fur, but for her oval face, her buttocks, and the palms of her hands. If she was my treasure, Dung Baba feared and hated her; as he picked his teeth with his great knife, he plotted to kill us both. But Hornprick, who sees and hears everything, broke off a sharp piece of his crown. He gave it to Kishkishkat and bade him to cut out Dung Baba's heart. This heart—shaped like a European urinal—was no bigger than an onion. Tumbling to the floor, Dung Baba's body deflated like a bladder of spoiled wine.

We escaped to the Tower of Invention where the Devil sat waiting; his black crown, broken in countless places, stood as tall as a date palm upon his head. There he bestowed upon Naatiffe, Kishkishkat, and me the three infinite oceans, so that we might live in peace. And it is we who have parented all the gentle whales that inform the world with enchantment, sobriety, and tenderness. . . .

The Nipple

All his life Lenez had lived with his mother and now she was dead. He had womanized with the whores but nothing more, and why should he have thought of more—of marriage and (God forbid!) of children—when his mother had cared for him so amiably all those years. No other woman would have put up with his heavy drinking and rowdy friends, he was sure of that! But she had died (Why? Why had she left him, her own loving Georges, and so suddenly too?). How cruel was life, how terrible death; it had never occurred to Georges that his mother would someday die.

So stricken had he been that for two months he did not even look at a glass of wine, and what is more he had (for despite a certain spotty redness about the face and an overhanging belly he was still *bel homme*) conceived an amorous alliance with La Veuve Fromentin, inheritress of a prosperous fruit farm.

He had known her all his life, and what man's slumber had not been troubled by her luxurious image? How surprised, how pleased he had been when she had stopped him in the street, her basket filled with pears (*like little breasts!* he had thought and blushed), to ask him in her easy and straightforward manner (that at the time both frightened and excited him) if he could spare a moment and come to her—perhaps that very evening? Something to do with trees—he hadn't quite understood—but most willingly he had gone. To find her in the darkening kitchen, opulent of waxed cherry, gleaming in the last light of day.

She had been silent at first; with an elegantly languorous gesture had simply pointed to the chair where he was to sit (doubtless her defunct husband's chair—larger than the others and invitingly upholstered in a worn burgundy velvet). She had caught her breath and then quickly, in that throaty voice of hers, a deep brown voice that filled his head with visions of great disorderly beds, had said:

"They tell me you've been off the bottle since your mother's death, Monsieur, is this so?"

He hadn't thought about it! And had to admit with a start that *it was so!* He had been so low these past weeks as to actually have forgotten to drink! No wonder time had crawled by! How had he survived? But her question, and above all her *look*, had so enkindled him that assuming what had simply been a trick of fate he replied:

"*Oui*, Madame. Not a drop since her death that horrible morning when I found her dead. Her heart had stopped, I wonder why? One wonders why!" He searched her eyes for sympathy.

Sympathy she had; he was a strongly built man with a handsome, sensuous mouth and melancholy eyes; secretly she had always wanted him, certain that once wrenched from his dreadful mother's grasp he would be quite a catch.

"Georges . . ." she breathed, calling him by his first name for the first time, "Georges . . . I need a man."

And it had been that simple!

Somehow he had known enough not to kiss her, not yet, but to answer with both dignity and humility:

"If you think I am such a man, Madame, then perhaps I am."

And she, unable to bear the weight of the moment any longer, had thrown herself into his arms panting:

"Georges . . . I've always wanted you!"

And he, solemn as a mortician, had had the wit to answer:

"Me too. *C'est le destin!*"

It was the high point of his life. Perhaps it was destiny! Georges walked home in a state of shock, glee bubbling in his guts so irresistibly that he had peed several times in the dust before reaching the fusty house he had shared for too long with his mother. That night he thought about La Veuve Fromentin, *Fernande* Fromentin, *his* Fernande. The news hit the village like a bomb.

✸

Until their wedding day the lovers lived apart. Fernande wanted it that way; an experienced woman, she knew the value of waiting for desired objects. As for Georges, the time of mourning his mother was not quite over. At night, as eager as a very young girl, Fernande slipped into the cool deep of her great bed alone (alone! but not for long!) and hungered for her lover.

"Ah! J'ai envie de lui!" she cried to her breasts, cupping them in her soft hands. She fondled her breasts but nothing else. She was saving it all for Georges.

And Georges? He was out a lot, walking off his paunch and learning as much as he could about the management of fruit farms. Reading was for him a tedious business and every image of a forked tree brought Fernande's thighs to mind. But he tried his best and figured that anyway, it was only a matter of time before he'd be handling Fernande's trees with familiarity and savoir-faire. Besides, she had two workers on the place, two gnarled *types*; he'd show them who was boss but he'd know when to be humble; they'd teach him and with Fernande to inspire him—why he'd learn fast!

❉

The eve of his wedding, Georges invited his cronies to wine and dine at La Toison d'Or—a local café-restaurant wherein the very blonde Madame Saignée offered a succulent meal and a generous assortment of the fine local wines. This was to be Georges's first fling in months—as well as his last. The occasion was therefore both joyous and solemn.

Madame Saignée greeted the men with her usual ambivalence: a haughty look preceded a highly evocative swaying of the hips as she led them to a table shining immaculately in the center of the small dining room like a thing most holy. The men sat down in clamorous admiration before a large platter of *fruits de mer*—mussels, oysters, and crabs bedded down in seaweed that curled suggestively around the gaping shells. Obese in a spanking new wheelchair, Horace the cripple cupped a mussel in his right hand and frigged it with his left before slip-

66

ping it into his mouth with a satisfied howl. The first bottles of Chenin blanc were opened to the sounds of cheering; soon the dishes—heaped with shells and the rinds of gutted lemons—were cleared away and each man attacked a gilded whiting swimming in cream, its tail cunningly caught up in its mouth.

"That's some trick!" said Horace. "I wonder how he does it?"

"Loneliness . . ." Georges sighed, looking uncharacteristically pensive.

Horace bellowed: "Here come the virgins!"

La Saignée had brought out the new rosé. Puffing and perspiring she returned almost at once with the ducklings in their sauce of thyme, laurel, and green olives.

"Some spread!" someone gasped. "*Bordel!* What a feast!"

But Oscar, village rogue and dealer in fertilizers, complained that his duck was lacking her garters and stockings and shouted:

"Someone's been here before me!"

The raped ducklings, their fragile bones in mournful heaps, were soon forgotten; the cheese, stacked upon a board the size of a door, appeared coupled with a full-bosomed bottle of Champigny. But the pièce de résistance was a very sweet 1947 Anjou awakened from her deep slumber beneath a mossy but fragrant cork. It accompanied *la tarte Saignée*—a lush affair of ground almonds, pastry cream, flaky crust, and meringue.

From there they veered on to the *vin champagnisé*, and Lenez, who had not taken one drink during his entire courtship until now and feeling like the man he knew he really was, stood on his chair to sing the smutty songs of his youth, punctuated with small farts and windy toasts to Madame Saignée and her Toison d'Or. He even toasted Monsieur Saignée who, brooding behind the bar, grudgingly offered them a *fine*. It was then that Georges received his gift: a porcelain baby bottle filled with cognac and crowned with a bright rubber nipple.

✳

Georges had seen the object once before in the front window of a local *épicerie* and had wondered if any man had ever fallen so low as to take that bottle to bed. And if he laughed and joked with his pals about the gift, he thought of Fernande and his mood clouded over. He was growing mean (as so often when *cuité*). Smelling his darkening temper as a mare smells a storm, Madame Saignée told him firmly that it was time for him and his pals to go. After much grumbling, cursing, and jostling of chairs, Lenez and his crowd pulled out of the café and stumbled onto the street where—all in a faltering row—they passed gas and peed profusely together.

The next morning Lenez awoke fully dressed in a damp bed still clutching the bottle of cognac. His head hurt and his tongue filled his mouth like a huge portion of stale goat cheese; he could barely open his eyes. He saw the bottle and blinked and the red nipple—tucked beneath its cellophane wrapper— winked familiarly back at him. Seized by a terrific thirst, Lenez tore away at the cellophane and put the nipple to his lips.

"Maman!" he whispered, clutching the bottle and sucking hard, *"Maman!"*

✳

Patiently, in a silver dress, Fernande waited for Georges in front of the church. When at last she left her family and friends behind to find him, he was still fast asleep. Georges growled at Fernande when she tried to pull the nipple from his lips.

Fydor's Bears

Fydor was a small man and he hunted bears. He knew everything there was to know about them: by the shape and size of a footprint read the age, weight, and speed of an animal; he knew their seasons of amorous encounters and the wild gardens they haunted for honey. And the bears knew Fydor: his tics, his tenacity, and his peculiar smell—rancid as old fat forgotten at the bottom of a can.

Still Fydor was the more cunning. By the roots of windblown trees he dug deep traps and made them secret beneath weavings of bracken and leaves. Many times in the passing of the year would a bear sink with a nauseating thud to be stung by Fydor's arrows, enfevered with sleep, and hauled off to one of the many stout cages he kept in a cellar called home.

❋

Fydor hated his bears yet could not live without them. Their intimate habits, their torments and hungers excited him, sickened him, obsessed him. He thrived in the stench of their fur, their urine, and their tears.

And in time the bears became obsessed with Fydor. Locked into their cages like flies in amber, they turned to him—for he was the only thing they could turn to. They watched him, memorized his habits: the way he shuffled across the littered floors, or held a pan of water beneath a tap. In time the bears knew Fydor better than a woman knows her man after sharing a half century of boredom and bed. And as alchemists fool with foul matter changing colors and structures, the bears—woolly and immense—entered into Fydor's dreams and changed Fydor.

Night after night they lumbered down the narrow passages

of Fydor's mind to browse its rag stalls, its cut-rate china shops, leaving droppings, making drafts, causing sunset changes. They brought burdens of flowers, of fire; as at a shrine, they drugged the air.

And vines grew inside Fydor's mind, and halls of green shadow; lean hills, red earth, and places of perpetual picnic. Fydor's skull—barren before—sprouted grass. His dim, fly-ridden eyes grew luminous. Bears were now coursing through his blood, inhabiting his heart, his liver, his testicles.

His nerves writhed bears. His skin crawled bears. His bowels groaned: *Bears!* His cock yearned: *Bears!* He ate, slept, dreamed, fucked, and defecated bears until waking in a frenzy of longing, his eyes wild and circling the room like bears on bicycles, he ran to them, his pants bulging with longing and with keys. Fingers trembling, he found the locks and set them free to lumber off into the night.

And Fydor followed them. With a gruff expression of joy half human, half brute, followed his makers into the forest. Another beast among beasts; perhaps less agile, less ferocious perhaps. . . .

CREAM

OR, The Holy Trinity in the Kingdom of Heaven

This is my secret, sacred and sublime: each night Billy Cox comes to see me. Billy Cox of TV fame and internationally idolized caresses me, calls me his sweet sister I shouldn't tell but oh—one day they will see I am blessed by Divine Desire to see in 3-D what they do not dare dream: the Fragrant Gardens of Paradise, Venomous Hell, and Yes: The End Of The World *Hallelujah!*

APPEARING EACH NIGHT an Angel of Light his loins luminous exorcising evil darkness bathed in blue fire resplendent his guitar crusted with chalcedony his tongue anointing the tips of my breasts my heart melting Billy's music rocking me to sleep:
Lavender blue dilly, dilly—Lavender green
When I am King dilly, dilly—You'll be my Queen. . . .

✳

He is so *warm*. The Warmest Man I Have Ever Known—my bed a brazier, my belly a hearth HEAVENLY His Magic Wand so POWERFUL he rides an ardent stallion crimson thick and hard it burns but honeyed his torrid sugarplum and I'll just take it into my mouth his licorice whisper the magic words and grow new teeth impeccable my skin apricots fresh from Olympian Orchards and the moss on my pubis lustrous hummingbird wing My Sweet Lord My Tender Jesus I'll be the Queen of Heaven make me Pope make my digestion work perfectly my hair a bush burning in gold lamé mantle floating on my shoulders— THE SKY WILL SPLIT OPEN LIKE A MELON. When they see how magnificent they will know just who I am! Din of Despair Everywhere—Envy thick as grass. They will fall to their knees to lap the dust at my feet imploring Mercy. THERE IS NO MERCY.

FOR I AM THE POWER
AND THE GLORY
FOR I AM THE FLOWER OF THE FLOCK: CREAM.

＊

That day will come Triumphant. Billy Cox of TV fame and Internationally Idolized will lift me in his arms then
   Together we will soar silver birds above the mud
   BEINGS IMMACULATE dazzling
   burnished by Holy Kisses glowing with the GRACE of the Holy Ghost to join Jesus an Enchanted Embrace tucked into the Milky Way He will pull aside the Curtain of Thorns and the Sheet of Fire—show us the damned nailed to Hell hollering for Grace. THERE IS NO GRACE!
   OH BILLY! We will be Lords of the Sky! Oh Billy! Just You and Jesus and I!
   Blue sky   royal blue   azure   cerulean
   CELESTIAL BLISS! KINGDOM OF HEAVEN!
   KINGDOM OF ME!
   oh Billy
   I am
   coming—

Luggage

The day after Emily Beth died her husband Charles went shopping. He took the silver-blue Starfire Road Burner he'd bought from Comet Cars on the Straightway. The car still smelled of wax and rubber and clean ashtrays; Charles, freshly bathed and in a new autumn gold jacket, lit up a slim Torpedo Queen.

He turned onto the Straightway and approached the Gilded Smile Shrimp and Lobster Paradise. Emily Beth and he had often eaten here, before her sickness when she had still been his dear girl with an appetite that matched his own. His sadness transformed itself quickly into hunger; years before his heart and stomach had united to become one and the same organ—his precious paunch, his pouch, his darling wallet, his pocket, his pail for love and dinner—his hamper.

He turned on the radio. The music slipped gracefully into his throbbing hamper and swelled it; he turned into the Gilded Smile and entering Little Boy Blue's Corner washed his hands. He looked into his face which had not changed since Emily Beth's death except perhaps for the line beside the corner of his mouth that had deepened.

Charles ordered an early lunch; he had not slept much the night before and he hoped the food would wake him up. When it came it was perfect—just the way he and Emily Beth had liked it—always the same, exactly the same texture, color, and taste. His hamper felt rocked, loved, full, grateful. "Here's to you, darling," said Charles, waving a small pink shrimp on the tip of his fork at no one across the table. Emily Beth would not have approved of the dessert—a great and glorious glob of vanilla-butter crunch on a piece of rhubarb pie. But of course, under the circumstances, she would have understood his weakness. "I know you understand, darling," thought Charles. "Bless you,

---

little girl." And his hamper welled up with tears not so much in sorrow but in gratitude. The bill paid, the tip left beside the plastic cactus on the table, he brushed crumbs from his jacket and made it back to the Straightway. In two minutes he had turned into Drug Bug Podium.

Charles had a nice collection of toilet water but he wanted to buy something called Socrates, which was advertised "For the older man: a scent that speaks of wisdom and the golden richness that only the years can bring." Now that Emily Beth was dead and he both older and wiser, this seemed just the sort of smell he wanted to have for himself. His others—the Javanese Joy, the Salty Sailor, Safari Scent, and Orphic Orange—were no longer right for him. Not that he had changed, heaven forbid. He had deepened, ripened even—Emily Beth had deepened, ripened him by dying. No, it would be sacrilegious—yes sacrilegious to smell like something that called itself Salty Sailor at such a moment. Emily Beth would have approved of his purchase, he was sure of it. The salesgirl, a sharp, lovely thing with jet black hair and *moonlitperl* skin, sprayed a sample of Socrates onto his wrist. Yes, there was a certain "golden richness" to it. A certain subtle dignity. And he thought that his choice of shrimp for lunch had been undignified; for dinner he would have something less frivolous, for example roast beef, and no silly dessert. Dear Emily Beth! Now he understood—it was not only health that had worried her so—doubtless she had considered the problem of his desserts as a problem in aesthetics. A "ripened" man, a "deepened" man—a man, in short, like Socrates—does not eat ice cream. A modest slice of cheese, a piece of fruit—these are the things a man of wisdom chooses for dessert.

Hugging his small parcel to his infant organ, his darling hamper that nestled within him like a fetus full of promise and discovery, he walked down the aisles of Drug Bug Podium pleased to see that he already had, in the vast chrome and marble medicine cabinet at home, everything he wanted. He was pleased too that he had chosen so wisely—there was no reason to waste time here. He went out and crossed over to the Regal Male Men's Shop. It occurred to him that none of

74

his shirts quite matched the handsome autumn gold of his new jacket, and that a man in his position should look harmonious. Charles looked down and saw to his horror that he was wearing a tie that had some sky blue in it—a terrible faux pas—sky blue and autumn gold were horrible together—an unforgivable mistake. What could have possibly come over him? He would have liked very much to go into the Regal Male to buy some shirts—the afternoon was clear and the funeral not until the next day—but he couldn't possibly wearing that terrible tie! Unless he took it off and explained to the salesman that he had spilled some gravy on it and wanted to buy a new one. He could take it off before going into the Regal Male and just drop it in a wastebasket.

Charles took off the tie and went into the Regal Male. It smelled wonderful in there—the refined smell of wool and leather, and the air was crisp. He wondered if they sprayed the air with something to make it crisp. His plan worked well; the jacket was obviously very expensive and the salesman did not seem to notice that Charles was not wearing a tie. He bought himself three cream-colored shirts and three wool ties—all had a touch of the fashionable autumn gold. He bought socks as well, and some shorts, and when he had finished he began to look forward to a shower, a new set of clothes, and a sober dinner of roast beef and cheese and a piece of fruit for dessert—figs or fresh grapes would be nice. On his way out of the Regal Male he passed Lion and Leather and went in to ask the price of a small wallet that caught his eye in the window. It was a "travel" wallet with a special pocket for credit cards and large enough for European currency. He remembered that his birthday was in two weeks and decided to get the wallet for himself. (He was certain that Emily Beth would have chosen just that; he would have told her about it over dinner—"Saw a very handsome wallet over at Lion and Leather. . . ." And she would have said, "A wallet? At Lion and Leather? Oh but darling, you don't need another wallet." And she would have gone out the very next day and bought it for him.)

His hamper swelled as he watched the salesgirl wrap the wallet up for him. He dawdled in the shop after, clutching

Socrates and the wallet together, and he found a clever week-end bag on sale with a carefully designed pouch for socks and another for toiletries. He bought it, though it intrigued him that he should have discovered this particular piece of luggage, on sale, with the specially designed pouches just after purchasing socks and toilet water.

"Emily Beth," he said aloud as he drove back home in the Starfire, "Emily Beth, I know you are there, watching me; that you, my darling wife, are now my dear guardian angel. You have ripened me by dying and deepened me, and in your own wifely and cunning way you led me to the weekend bag. Emily *girl*," he whispered, patting the tight leather seat beside him. And his hamper, packed with guilt and gratitude, snapped open, and for a time he wept.

Harriet

When she left the asylum, Harriet had no place to go. Mother, always charitable, took her in. She stayed in the spare room and was useful. She was thirty. And she had three eyes. Witch sisters, they branded her face with a raw and smoking triangle.

From the first moment I loved her. Loved her! I worshiped Harriet. Harriet was sex and Harriet was geometry. Twin stars they traced the same maddening orbit that sealed my brain with sperm and with fire. I was eight years old. On a large piece of cream-colored paper I drew this device:

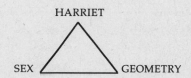

After dinner Harriet brought me a slice of cake. A triangle of dark chocolate, it looked just like Harriet's cunt. I ate cake and thought of Harriet. I ate Harriet and thought of cake. And tried to catch her crazy gaze in mine but never could, entirely.

I painted an eye on my forehead. Queen and servant, our madness and our magic there for everyone to see, we walked hand in hand in the city park. Desire burned brighter in me than the fire of a magic pentagon. I spent the entire afternoon painting an eye on my navel. Delirious, I ran to show Harriet. BUT SHE WAS GONE!

Gone! And she had told me nothing. Nothing! It had never occurred to me that Harriet suffered. That Harriet wanted to be like other women. Crazy Harriet! That morning she had gone to the clinic to have her eye removed. Removed! CUT OUT OF HER HEAD!

I lay in my bed and stared at the linoleum. Her eye—Harriet's eye—stared back at me. All day long it blinked at me like a mad owl in a tree. At night, a fragile egg, it nested in my pillow. It twinkled on the face of the moon.

Fed by my fever, Harriet's eye grew to gigantic proportions. Breathless, I watched as it transformed itself into an oyster, a diamond, an open mouth—the sea.

Her salty cunt spread over my face like the sky—foaming and smelling of the city park. I lapped lava as a cat skims cream from a dish. When at last my fever lifted, my brain was softer than butter that has been beaten with salt. My lips were iridescent, my skin transparent.

Six weeks later she was back—not a trace of the third eye on her forehead. NOT A TRACE! But far more terrible—the two remaining eyes WERE NOT HARRIET'S! Harriet was an IMPOSTER! The filthy bitch!

The others saw the difference.

Harriet—her head is preserved in oil and sits in the corridor of a famous hospital.

Harriet—her severed head is impaled on a post and stands at the gate of a splendid circus.

Harriet—each night her head multiplies itself a billion times and men, pointing to the bloody orbit transfixed by three immobile moons, marvel and whisper, "stars!"

Harriet—they put her to sleep and removed the eye. It slipped and rolled to the floor making the sound men call "thunder."

When it rains it is only Harriet who is crying.

Foxes

When I was a young girl I loved foxes. I lived in a time-worn and venerable mansion by the Hudson surrounded by woods thickening to forest—and there were foxes, slim-nosed, fast-tailed foxes; they could be seen in summer, a ruddy flash under brush, and in winter, a swift stain darting across the snow. But much as I longed to, I never got to know them; they were too fast, too secretive, and too busy. I imagined that their lives were complex and mysterious, undoubtedly color-ful; foxes the Gypsies of the animal kingdom—sly, quick, and achingly handsome. If I could have been transformed by a fairy godmother into something other than what I was, I would have chosen to be a fox.

I had two fantasies then: in the first I was Rebecca Redwing the Fox Queen, with the sweeping russet skirts and uncannily swift legs; in the second I was a mermaid with green scales and red hair—a sort of Norma Shearer transformed to water baby.

After my parents' white Daimler wrapped itself around a tree and I was forever banished from the big house by the river, I spent most of my time dreaming rather than being. My parents laid to rest, I was sent to Hoboken to live with my grandmother.

Grandma's apartment was very small. It boasted a gloomy foyer that even a large mirror could not broaden or lighten, a kitchen guarded by a gnomish refrigerator stacked with stale cans of Dole's pineapple-orange juice and little else, a living room with a view of traffic, quick-lunch counters, and seedy groceries, a tiny tiled bathroom with irritable drains, and a stuffy, grey-carpeted bedroom. Dwarfed beneath an immense black portrait of Grandmother as a young woman, we shared the lumpy bed.

Grandmother was Spanish and looked it: large, somber, wet

eyes, masses of dark hair, and a finely arched nose with delicately flaring nostrils. The lips, although passionate, were hard and unyielding and spoke of both the spoiled child and the bitter woman. It was a good painting but I could never know if it had captured her: she was too old, a wreckage of a woman with hardly any lips left at all. Her eyes, bedded down in creases, peered dim and guppylike from under the two fishbowls that were the lenses to her glasses.

✳

"Once I was so beautiful," she is fond of saying, "so beautiful, that men would hold their breath when I passed them by."

"Why did they hold their breath?" I ask.

"They saw me and their hearts stopped."

✳

My grandmother gives me breakfast—a jelly roll and a glass of Dole's pineapple-orange juice. She pads over to the fridge for some milk, brings it to the table, pours some into her coffee, sits down heavily in front of me, and sighs. For a few minutes we chew in silence, then she says:

"If it hadn't been for your no-good Hungarian grandfather and your lousy gambling daddy, I wouldn't be washing my own frigging floors!"

Ashamed, I look down at the dirty linoleum. Puffing up her cheeks she lets out a wet burst of fathomless despair:

PHOUTT!

After breakfast I clear the table as Grandma washes herself in the black and turquoise bathroom. When I put the coffee away I see a box of one of my mother's homemade fruitcakes. The box is spotted with rust and what is left of the Christmas tape is tarnished but I'm excited—there's a chance that I'll find something nice in there. I open the box but all I find is a tribe of very frightened roaches. Fighting nausea and terror I run from the apartment and throw the whole mess into the garbage chute. And listen to the sound of the metal box as it crashes down,

down, and the box *my body is falling down a well the unforgiving stones smeared from top to bottom with my darkest secrets. Broken long before my fall comes to an end I am as empty as an egg sucked clean by a snake. But what if I reach the bottom alive?*

"A miracle! She is still alive!"

Spiders live in wells, there are lots of them—their eight terrible eyes stuck around their heads like the jewels in my mother's tiara. Down there at the bottom of the well I am brave. I do not look at the spiders. I call for help:

"HELP!"

From out their secret mazes foxes leap; they have heard my cries and come running by the twos and threes, by the dozens, by the hundreds. Yelping they give me courage and when they reach the well they look down upon me kindly. I see their eyes above me shining like stars.

"MARIA THERESA!"

My grandmother calls from the apartment. She stands at the door, monumental in terry robe, hair wet, red slippers matted: Grandma the frazzled Aztec calling for blood. As I approach she slaps me hard across the face. I burst into tears.

"Why? Grandma! What have I done?"

She arches her head, her cheeks swell with venom, and she strikes:

"The fruitcake, you little shit!"

"There were roaches!"

"Roaches! In my apartment! My apartment is clean! No bugs! NO BUGS!"

A neighbor sticks her head out angrily into the hall:

"No bugs, HA!" she spits onto the carpet. "ALL the roaches in this place and you know where they come from! Number 94! EVERYBODY KNOWS!"

"You! Mrs. Chickenshit!" My grandmother rages, straddling an invisible pyramid: "Mrs. Chickenpiss! Stinking up the whole world with her frigging cabbage! THERE ARE NO BUGS IN MY APARTMENT. My own grandchild," she sobs, prodding the dead light bulb on the ceiling for sympathy, "a traitor in my own apartment!"

"Grandma," I plead as I follow her back inside, "that fruitcake was marked 1948, that made it five years old. FIVE YEARS OLD."

"So I was aging it. So you haven't heard of aged fruitcake?"

We go back into the kitchen and sit down. She makes herself another cup of coffee, digs into the ashtray for a good-sized butt, stretches it out carefully so as not to break the paper, cuts off the hard black end with her knife, finds that the knife has been used for butter, curses, wipes off the cigarette with her rumpled paper napkin, puts it into her mouth where it is immediately stained purple, and lights up. She coughs, tears come into her eyes, she strokes my cheek:

"My little jewel. So there were bugs? Yes, I believe you. You are a pretty girl, just like your old grandmother was—why should you be lying? Listen. This morning we'll do my hair, the grey is showing at the roots. We'll fix me up. A little red, a little black, and my girdle. . . . You'll put on your Easter coat, your red shoes—a little duchess! And we'll go to the fancy French pastry on Ninetieth Street and buy meringues, pistachio éclairs, anything you want! Would you like that?"

I say: "Yes. I would like that very much." Knowing that it's all a lie, that she'll never get herself into the elevator.

We go into the bathroom. She takes out the bottles: blue, black, and yellow; she sits on the little turquoise stool; I pour the contents of the first bottle onto her head; I rub it in, it smells terrible and makes me cough. She sends me running to the kitchen for another butt. I rummage through the ashtrays, find one, pull it into shape, scratch off the hard end, and light it for her. I suck on it—surprised by the burning smoke that tears into my mouth. I bring it to her, she takes it and grunts, "*Gracias*," smokes a minute in silence and adds:

"You know, once I smoked silver cigarettes. They were the most expensive kind—very smart! Come!"

She stands up, her hair in purple foam. I follow her into the bedroom. She goes to her closet and fishes around, pushing aside crippled high-heeled shoes, boxes of hoarded perfume, stockings rolled into balls, and a black leather dog leash. At last she uncovers a small flat box covered with flaking metallic paper and pulls it out.

"This is for you. Come! Open it in the bathroom."

Foam dribbles down her neck. She sits on the stool smoking and I on the edge of the stained bathtub. I open the box. Beneath the folds of tissue paper I find a pair of green gloves. Delicate rosebuds, serrated leaves, and fluid stems are embroidered at the wrists.

"They were mine." And raising her twisted arthritic hands: "I can't wear them anymore." She tries to laugh.

I sit on the edge of the tub looking at the gloves, turning them like pages back and forth, not knowing how to thank her. They are as fine as spiderweb and the color of the sea . . .

A great lady rides through the forest in a swift green coach, her hand delicately poised beside the open window. It is spring and the woods on either side of the road teem with life. Foxes come out from behind the trees to see the woman pass—the witch woman with red hair and green eyes, wearing the most beautiful gloves. They come in droves and run beside the coach, yelping.

A young fox asks his father: "Who is it?"

"It is Rebecca Redwing, our Queen!"

"It is She, father!"

"Yes, my son, it is She."

From the bed the young girl my grandmother was watches me; her thin lips flutter and I seem to hear her whispering— something about demons concealed beneath flowers and fingers stitched, stitched to the butcher's block.

The Radiant Twinnie

We are the twinnies, Lolly and I, but I am the radiant twinnie. I have always been the radiant twinnie. Lolly will be an old maid, Mother said it, but I will be snatched up like a sticky bun.

Lolly was the second one to come out. I slipped out like a dream but Lolly stayed stuck—a nasty red brick cemented to Mother's tender tummy—Mother will *never* forgive her. They had to pry Lolly loose. As a baby I never cried and my appetite was terrific. They had to force-feed Lolly. In fact they had trouble keeping her alive. Her eyes have never changed—baby blue and cold as igloos. Mine are like Mother's—a warm brown with long lashes. Lolly *never* looks anybody in the eyes.

We share the same room—though Mother says I simply *must* have my own soon and course she is right. I can't spend my entire life with that freak Lolly. What did it was the box of Modesty. Mother bought us each some for *when the time comes*. Mother says it could be any day now. My breasts are tender— I asked Lolly if *her* breasts were tender but all she said was: "Cut the crap." I know she's jealous because I am bound to have *my* curse before she does—in fact Mother says it will be a miracle if Lolly isn't *sterile*. Actually she took us to the doctor's to find out. He looked at me and told Mother that I was *flawless and radiant*. But when it was Lolly's turn to go in she screamed and screamed and wouldn't let the doctor go anywhere near her! It was a *terrible* scene, really *embarrassing*, and Mother slapped Lolly several times. Well that shut her up. When we got home she locked her in the *bathroom* and Lolly had to sleep in the *bathtub*. And the faucet leaks so Lolly got a cold—but I know she got sick on purpose to make us feel sorry. Anyway who could be sorry after what she did? Boy is she ever *dumb*. She tore open her box of Modesty and shredded it all over the

84

room screaming that she didn't ever want any perverted doctor poking around inside her—and Mother said: "If you keep this up, Lolly, you're going to turn into a frigid woman," and Lolly said: "That's OK just as long as I don't have a frigid head like yours, Mother!"

When Daddy came home and heard what Lolly had said he called her into his office and gave her a terrible spanking though she is almost thirteen, and that's when she got her *period*. When Daddy realized what had happened he got very upset and emotional and I heard him ask Lolly to forgive him. And do you know what she said? She said: "Father, it is too late for me to forgive anyone in this house!"

I ran to the kitchen and told Mother. You can imagine how angry she was. But she was very calm. She reminded Lolly that she would be dead now if it hadn't been for her and what a terrible baby she had been and how much she had made Mother suffer! And all that time Lolly just sat there with this awful smirk on her face looking at the plastic tablecloth. Then my daddy came in and said: "Let's leave Lolly alone now, I think we have all been picking on her too much. Now that Lolly is a young woman we must treat her like one." But I said: "No, she isn't a real woman! She's frigid and nasty and I hate her!" And Daddy got very red and I was afraid he was going to hit me! My daddy! But he just told me to go to my room.

Months have passed and Lolly has already gone through four boxes of Modesty. Mine is still intact—shiny in its cellophane. The red pull tab is still tightly wound around the top. The last time Lolly was cursed I was certain that she was *pretending* just to make me jealous. So I went into the bathroom and looked into the wastebasket. There was real blood—but I wondered if maybe Lolly had cut herself to make it *look* like she was bleeding *from there?* That's when I decided to look at her body when she was sleeping because she never lets me see her naked—ever. I opened up the door and put on the hall light very quietly, and I was careful to pull the covers back gently so that she wouldn't wake up. She was wearing panties. I had to admit that her body is OK. In fact her breasts are a little bigger than mine. I looked her over carefully but I didn't see a cut anywhere.

85

Suddenly I saw Lolly's crazy eyes staring at me in the dark. They were like cat's eyes by the side of the road shining yellow except that hers are blue.

"If you ever look at my body again I will kill you," she said.

Just like that. So I moved out—down to the pantry closet. I took Granny Hanna's quilt with me and Teddy and my film magazines. Daddy smiled when he saw what I was doing and said: "What a great idea, Helen!" But Mother was furious and said: "It's Lolly who should be in the pantry—not you!" But I said: "No—I really like it here." Lolly got up late and didn't say anything except: "Get your crap out of the dresser." So I went back up and got my stuff and that shitty box of Modesty. I *wish* Mother had saved it for when I'll really *need* it. It made me feel so—*humiliated.*

Mother has been strange lately. Could Lolly have said anything to her? Well what is so *awful* about looking at my own sister's *body?* Lolly never talks to Mother though. So it must be that other thing. Yesterday she said: "It's strange that you still haven't had your period yet, Helen. And Lolly is wearing a bra now—and your titties are not developing. I think we had better see the doctor." But I said: "Mother! The last time he said that I was flawless! FLAWLESS AND RADIANT!"

The appointment is for next Friday after school.

The Double

When Mrs. Bloomgarden awoke at seven o'clock on Saturday morning the third of September, she discovered that her feet had come off sometime during the night. Small and sympathetic, her feet had tumbled to the floor and lay quietly on the rug—their fresh pink nail polish shining prettily in the sun.

"Well, I'll be damned!" she exclaimed. And turning to Leo Bloomgarden she whispered, perhaps more harshly than she intended, "Leo! Wake up for God's sake; wake up, Leo!"

"I'm leaving," said Leo simply after breakfast. "Forgive me, Gloria, but I can't take it." "Poor Leo," she said, stroking the back of his neck. "Don't throw them out," he indicated the bedroom as he left. "Who knows? They might come in handy," and he chuckled.

"That Leo," she smiled to herself after he had gone. "Always ready for a laugh"

*

The next day she noticed that her feet were growing back. With a pang of secret understanding she went to find the shoe box hidden in the closet. In a moment her feet lay bare and vulnerable in her lap. She smiled. It was as she had thought. No, she was not surprised—hadn't she known all along? The feet were growing legs.

"Will they join?" she pondered. "I suppose I'd better leave them out of the box now." She lay them on the bed, being careful to place them in proper juxtaposition. If they were going to join, as undoubtedly they were (were not her own feet now half grown back?), there would be no malformation. And that is why, within a very short time, a new Gloria Bloomgarden grew perfectly and to full height. (I shudder to think what might have happened had she left her feet in the shoe box. . . .)

That night she lay in bed beside the new Gloria (who had not yet attained consciousness) and watched her sleep. "How beautiful I am," she thought. She bent over the sleeping double and kissed her on the lips. "When she awakens tomorrow" (and it was certain she would awaken—were not her own two feet fully regrown but for the nails?), "when she awakens I will not tell Leo," she decided. "I will keep her to myself. She will be my secret as I will be hers. How lovely it is going to be!" Gently she caressed the double's perfect breasts (beneath which she distinctly heard the beating of a heart).

Spanish Oranges

Madame Magot owns the ancient butcher and grocery shop that festers shamelessly in front of the cathedral. Among other things she sells fresh beef, factory-made sausages, dog food, blood pudding, and chewing gum. She does so much business she has had to take on Clara, an unwed mother with acne and astigmatism, to sit at the cash register.

Today cow heart is on sale and the store stews with blowsy housewives, irritable and morose, who feed on headcheese, packaged ham, and store-bought cake.

Old man Magot is mad. He has been to Saint Felix, the local loony bin, so often Madame has lost count. The last time they took him away it had been *terrible* and she certain to be rid of him for good—good riddance! He had peed all over the ambulance. But here he is back again, standing in a corner, eyeing the customers and sucking on an orange. It is just before Christmas, the Spanish oranges are dog-cheap, the pockets of his pants are bulging with them, he can eat them all day, it keeps him busy— she does not care what it is he does with himself as long as it keeps him busy. However, old man Magot is not satisfied merely eating his oranges and soon, with fatal glee betrayed by the fecal glint in his eyes, he throws an orange peel at one of the customers, a frumpish mother of nine packed into a rayon housedress. As she bends over her frazzled basket to nest a bag of eggs, a peel hits her on the head. Clara giggles behind a stubby hand and Madame, with dead eyes and clenched teeth, slices viciously into the cow heart. The hair on her chin bristles. If she could think of a way to kill him cleanly she would, but she can't.

It is noon. As the church bell rings, the siren screams from the roof of the *mairie*. With sighs and secret farts the women leave the store. Clara crosses the street to her rented room for a warmed-over dish of cauliflower and Madame starts upstairs to cook the inevitable grey-green slop dubbed *potage vert* for lunch. She tells old man Magot to follow her but he refuses and, all at once giddy, throws a handful of orange peels into her face. Imitating the cheap cuts under the counter she turns purple and cursing "Scurf! Ulcer! Hogwash! Negro!" slams heavily up the stairs.

Old man Magot is alone. A parrot on a perch, he balances on one foot, then another, and pulls an orange from his pocket. Lovingly he caresses it, snuffles it, peels it; tosses a curl of skin at a side of mutton, another into the bowl of headcheese on the counter, at the stack of canned dog food, the dangling sausages, the gaping wad of cow heart that seeps darkly onto its yellowed porcelain tray. The air fries with the festive smell of citrus, the polecat fug of pesticides. Dreamily he throws the peeled orange at the floor. *Plop!* It leaves a small mess. Madame calls him for lunch. He doesn't move. She calls again. Threats and curses. "Jew! Bedpan! Cretin! Dwarf!" She stamps down the stairs to fetch him.

Madame peers into the shop. Can't see him anywhere—he must be hiding. *Plop!* The orange bounces off her forehead and rolls under the counter. She takes a step into the room. *Plop!* Another—this time thrown hard and aimed at her stomach. She is frightened. She doesn't speak to him; she knows it is impossible to try. Instead she speaks to God. God help me. God deliver me from this madman, this bedpan I have for a husband. God give me patience. *Plop!* The orange smashes into her temple. God be damned! *Plop! Plop! Plop!* This time she gets it in one eye, the temple again, her forehead. She screams. "Dog! Dirty rat! Worm! Abortion!"

Plop! The orange hits her on the mouth; her lip splits against her teeth. Sucking blood she sees him stooping behind the stacked dog food. His hands and pockets are empty. He gapes at her stupidly. She thinks: it's over. And edges towards him. He picks up a can. *No!* But she gets it *Wham!* in the belly. *Wham! Wham! Wham!* In the head, in the belly, in the chest. *Crack!* He has hit her in the head again, hard. He's going strong now, thrusting with all his force. Looking happy. Madame falls.

Madame is lying on the floor, twisting, moaning, sawdust sticking to her face, her sweater. A can tears into her back. *Thwack!* He is a boy again, laughing, smashing plaster Chinamen at the fair. *Thwack! Thwack! Thwack! Thwack!* He picks up the bowl of headcheese and throws it at her, then the sausages, the jars of pickles, olives, the canned tripes, the sliced steak, the clotted heart and its tray. He pours out the bottles of olive oil, of vinegar and violet wine.

✳

Bells. One. Two. Opening time. Dragging his feet, he fumbles with the keys and unlocks the door. Clara comes in. She sees him crouching behind the counter and giggles. Then she sees the mess. Gasping, she runs to the stairs. "Madame! Madame!"

Old man Magot seizes Clara. It is incredible how strong he is, this man who for years has not been able to wash himself or cut his own meat. He pins her against the counter and rams her glasses down her throat. With his free hand he gropes for a small salami. He rams and pushes until nothing more will go down and Clara has slipped lifeless to the floor. Grunting he lifts her up and hangs her by the collar of her coat from a silver hook that swings in the air like a claw. Then he unbuttons his pants and pees on her, the floor, the cans of food, Madame.

He is very tired. Breathing hard, he locks the door. Then padding back to the counter, he sweeps away the meat and climbs inside. It is cold. The cold feels good. Cradling his head with his arms he falls asleep. He lies as still as Snow White beneath the glass, shreds of poisoned fruit caught in her teeth.

The Beast

I live in the beast's belly. I nourish and sleep there. She is kind to me. She is tender and warm.

The day she came to devour me I saw that her eyes were good and her teeth soft. I was not afraid and let her swallow me, whole like an olive.

"You will be happy," I heard her say as I rolled down her throat, slippery and wet. Like a bird I set to work immediately upon a nest of leaves and shredded fern and bedded down.

At day she sleeps and her belly is clouded over and quiet. At night she hunts (she prefers the flesh of small birds, their iridescent eggs, and beetles). When she is fed and happy she purrs like any large cat. When she is in heat she sings like a siren in the sea.

I live in her belly and I am happy. And if I have seen her face but once, I love it more than my life. She is my good beast and I am her son—her unborn godchild, her parasite.

Parasites
or, The Grocer's Wife

Deftly, if unintentionally, the barber removed a wart that had been aggravating me for years. Now all that remains of it is a small square of adhesive.

The barber paid, I dropped in at the grocery. The grocer is a sourpuss but his wife is ripe and appetizing. I told her I wanted smoked oysters. These she can reach only after climbing a collapsible metal ladder and still she has to stretch. At such moments her breasts dangle; the four straps of brassiere and slip cut deeply into the tender shoulders that shimmer beneath a translucent blouse.

✳

An unusually filthy dog sleeps in a corner of the shop. He has parasites and the nasty habit of making bad smells. The grocer's wife puts up with it as her husband is impotent and they have no children.

✳

Back home in my bachelor's kitchenette! My dinner plate sparkles on the table and looks very like a marine biologist's tray of specimens, brimming with soft things plucked from the belly of the deep. I imagine that I am a marine biologist preparing slides for the microscope as I place an oyster on a cracker. But instead of going under the microscope, the cracker goes into my mouth.

✳

I take an early bath. The water is warm and pleasant—I relish warm water immensely. I imagine that the bathwater is the sea and that I am a large white iceberg. A lonely iceberg floating in water many fathoms deep. A white island riddled with fauna: nesting penguins and their eggs, gulls, and walruses. Undoubtedly all these creatures sustain parasites of some kind —certainly they do—lice or fleas of a species suited to the bitter climate. Perhaps these little parasites sustain parasites—yes, surely they do! In any case, if I have parasites myself, by now they have drowned in the bath.

I give myself a terrific sudsing. I needn't wash my hair; the barber took care of that before he unintentionally removed the wart.

A wart is a parasite of sorts. A barren island, its root traveling deep beneath the flesh; a wrinkled volcano poised above a rosy sea. Often I think that you and I are but infinitesimal creatures clinging to some fool wallowing in a bathtub. Sooner or later some clown will start sudsing *and then where will we be?*

✺

I pat myself dry and put on fresh pajamas. God knows I need sleep. A hot bath, a good rest—and the nerves unravel like spools of thread rolling across a soft carpet. Everything is simple—now that I know what my Saltine Sheeba, my Queen of Queens, the succulent woman of my dreams wants me to do. For you see, this evening when she gave me my groceries, *she handed me a gun.*

The dog will have to go first, the grocer after. This much is clear. But one question remains to trouble me: Where will the dog's parasites go once he is dead? Will they migrate in silent swarms to the grocer's body? And once I have killed him? *Where will they go then?*

Sorrowing Rachilde

Her name is Rachilde. She is mocked in the hamlet of Cix for her intact hymen and her limp. She is approaching fifty. She likes to stand uncovered in the rain, a thing thought peculiar even in a child. But she is not often watched. She is too old and queer and grey. As she lopes along neglected in the streets, the young women shudder, should they see her, and promise themselves never to age the way Rachilde has. Anyway, she was always ugly, poor thing. They add *poor thing* in case God exists and is listening. But who cares? Isn't she an Arab or a Jewess with such a name?

In her father's house there is a clock in every room. The faces of his clocks, like the face of his aging daughter, were unknown to him. Thanks to his blindness, Rachilde was, until he died, ever young. Because she had never married, her father felt guilty and grateful. Often he said:

"Rachilde, a man will want you for your beauty and your limp. An intelligent man will know your limp will keep your beauty safe beside him." Her father was the only man who had called her beautiful. The one man who took her, and left her barren, never spoke of beauty or of wanting.

Once she took a bus to Angers where she bought her father a clock with a voice. The clock was a black cube and wireless, truly a thing of sorcery. The old man was delighted and always kept it close at hand. But the small electronic voice startled her when, passing through the wall, it roused her in the middle of the night. She gave it to the curé when her father died.

✳

The curé pays Rachilde two hundred francs a week to keep his rooms tidy and to wash his linen. Despite his clean, uncomplicated life, the curé produces a large quantity of dirt. He is pleased to have found an ugly Jewess to see to his basic needs. Rachilde prepares simple meals for him and leaves them warming at the corner of the oil stove along with a pot of fresh coffee. The curé loves her leek and potato soup and lamb stew. He does his marketing himself on a mufflerless motorized bicycle. He has bought an Italian machine to make ice cream.

✳

Rachilde suffers greatly. She aches with love and sorrow for everyone and everything, and her pain, a constant flame, illuminates the hamlet of Cix like a lantern. Rachilde is like a saint skinned alive and smiling, offering her heart to hounds.

Around her the hamlet hums like a hive; she sees the young girls blossom and marry and thicken; she sees the youths burnished by hunger grow bitter behind the counter at the grocery and the desk at the notary's and in the fields; she sees them lose fingers in the cannery and limbs on the highway, or die of self-inflicted wounds beside the overpriced bodies of metal automobiles they cannot meet the payments for. She sees all this and suffers, and if her own life has no swiftness, her heart counts the hours of the lives of others speeding past. The fragility, the futility of all things human and divine keep her sorrowing. Without discrimination she weeps over kittens, the untried beauty of babies, the green-ember scarabs stealing through the shadows in the garden after dark. Her sorrow is her only child.

It hurts Rachilde to see mothers buying powdered milk and rubber nipples at the pharmacy. Her own mother was a Gypsy, flighty and dark, affectionate and scatterbrained. Years ago she had run away, leaving behind the smell of smoke. Had Rachilde functioning breasts, she would gladly suckle all newcomers. No cord had bound her to the body of a baby, yet Rachilde reveres the cord that binds all things and when she weeps, Rachilde weeps milk. Her sorrow is a needle of fire. With it Rachilde repairs the tears in the braided fabric of the world.

✳

96

In her father's garden, Rachilde stands for hours enchanted by the vines that scrawl across the paths and tumble from the walls. Although they invade the garden, she cannot pull them out. Their flowers have no fragrance but their colors are tender, as pink as flesh. In late summer the perfumes of mint and lavender oil the air and when Rachilde stands in the rain, she is showering in volatile essences. In dry weather the locusts gather near and scraping their wings together like sticks send the crackling sound of fire up into the air. The sound reminds her of her mother's brittle hair. Running from some dark terror, a hedgehog collides into her and buries his face in the folds of her dress. But if people shun Rachilde it is because they know she is more than she seems to be, magical; perhaps they sense her work is titanic and that she should not be disturbed. Perhaps her sorrow shames them, or simply, they fear her limp, her solitude, her loving attitudes.

Alone, she gives herself to cats as lonely women do, talks to the garden toads, and feeds the ravens. She does not scold the cats when they kill because she has long understood the violent nature of the world and knows the cats are only listening to their inner clocks as those mothers in the pharmacy are not. She sees the cats birthing, purring all the while; she sees them eat the caul and swallow the cord. She sees the kittens suck, taking their time. All this tenderness and savagery makes her sad.

Alone and neglected, standing in the rain or in her father's house surrounded by silent clocks, a shadow too plain to count, too old to see, Rachilde holds the pulsing cord of the hamlet of Cix in her hand. It is her sorrow that keeps things going. The swallows return each spring because so much cheerfulness moves her to tears, and the bodies of lovers quicken because her own blood leaps as she holds their youth tightly to her heart. It is her queerness, her quickness, her limping, leaping love that precipitates the rain. The stars race across the sky because Rachilde stands beneath, sorrowing.

HOFRITZ

Death row, fourteen compartments, pinewood and clear glass; a moth in each cell. Once, looking on as a coffin was being laid in the ground, Hofritz had heard a voice intone:

That's where the moths go.

It was at that moment he had understood—his love of dead moths was simply a love of death in disguise.

❋

Upon occasion a moth escapes him, and if after a clumsy run he manages at last to hold it beating beneath his net, he will in a rage tear off its wings. His collection is small; Hofritz is not agile and his temper is bad. But those fragile corpses that do sleep in his white box are beauties so perfect they need only be kissed to return to life.

❋

Hofritz also collects what he calls *desperate relationships*. Years ago, as his wife's coffin was being lowered into the ground, he realized that *joie de vivre* was a thing alien to him, as was tenderness and, for that matter, pleasure.

❋

As a child, Hofritz had never played games for fear of winning. He still wants to pass through life as unobtrusively as possible. He does not want to be chosen in any way, to be outstanding or even *likable*. Secretly he admires the earthworm. And yet. . . .

❋

Hofritz studies the chrysalis and recognizes the cunning shape of the sleeping King. There is a clue to be had from the study of moth and King; both leave the husk transformed. King remains King, but of a new dimension; and moth, although he goes nowhere, wakens transformed to another self. How curious the voyages of the atoms of the self. Sepulture as athanor!

✳

In the past, Hofritz had feared change. People who change stand apart from the rest; they are visible. And he had wanted to be like the earthworm, eating dirt, making dirt, sameness before and behind. He had admired the invisible brotherhood of worms, each individual as alike as blades of grass or grains of sand. But now Hofritz studies the Kings and the chrysalis and considers them as clues to a deeper vision. When the chrysalis is metamorphosed into a moth, something of its primary caterpillar nature remains—if hidden. Just as the dead King hunting geese in the fragrant marshes of Paradise is still a King. With a pang, Hofritz realizes that beneath the husk of Hofritz, he is himself a King.

✳

Hofritz considers his husk. It is made of many layers. He removes the overcoat (for how long has he been standing in the kitchen staring at the tiled floor and talking to himself?). Blood seeps from beneath the grocery bag—his dinner. He removes his vest, his shirt, pants, shorts, undershirt, and socks— all the while admiring a spider that balances above the sink. With a shudder, Hofritz remembers that spiders do not wrap themselves up as he does, but only what it is they want to eat. And he wonders if his desire for change is not simply a desire for self-anthropophagy.

Sleep

I need old people because they put me to sleep, and for years I have had trouble sleeping. Not that I actually fall asleep in their company, but an old man's babbling rocks me, soothes me, and I find peace.

After a particularly difficult night I paid Maurice a visit. Maurice is a voluble gentleman in his late seventies who, the result of a stroke, has lost the use of his left arm. It lies limply at his side, and the hand, as plump and pink as a young woman's, sprouts from his sleeve: a tender bud, a rose of sugar. As Maurice speaks I suck on a cigar and look fondly at that useless hand. Its effect on me is hypnotic. Ah! The lovely member dead to all activity! I speak to my heart:

"Be twin to this hand! Be still!"

Maurice talks. It does not matter to me what he says. The important thing is that he ask nothing of me. Not even that I listen. So that I may sit in silence, deep in my comfortable chair, and let the sight of his hand—my precious, immobile talisman—and the patter of his words falling—a gentle, tepid rain—caress and hold me in a charm that counterfeits deep sleep, and from which I arise as from a clear pool.

Maurice's apartment is well suited to my needs—the perfect complement to his person. Everything he owns reflects the helpless state of his hand: the books bound in soft red leather and stored in the glass-fronted bookcase are locked in like so many bits of coral seized in a glass paperweight. And there is so much bric-a-brac accumulated there—teacups too fragile or too precious for use, jade figures, ivory elephants, slave bracelets—that should the doors be one day unlocked, it would be impossible to reach the books. (Oh blessed inactivity!)

The table upon which my cognac is served is waxed beyond credibility; its surface is shielded by a lace cloth in turn protected by three small doilies; the floor is blanketed by a profusion of Chinese carpets and rugs, and the maid crosses the room as silently as an angel crosses Heaven. All this scenery is wonderfully conducive to my psychic rest. The liqueurs gleam in their carafes, the pralines glow in their gilded paper.

"Never stop! Never stop!" I pray as I thrill to the murmur of Maurice's idiotic babbling. He utters enormities: the man is a bigot and a fool. But no matter. He is fitted to my need as his chair to my body. He speaks on and on; I am as content as a cat before the fire, a baby at the breast. No, I do not nod off, but sit frozen in a gesture of attention, a figure of jade. The magic is complete; my inner landscape is a calm pool, my body a bottle, my spirit—so troubled the night before—as still as those liqueurs in their carafes of crystal. His hand nests in his lap. Ah! My pink doll! My nerveless puppet!

Now that I have leisurely taken in the entire room, and relished in the contemplation of the hand, been rocked by the monotony of Maurice's babblement, I raise my eyes with some difficulty to his old scrubbed face. A smile on my lips, the smile of a bloated baby in a magazine, I admire his perfectly shaven face and neck, the silver hair combed into place, the faded eyes that demand neither answer nor recognition, the mouth. He never breaks the rhythm of his speech to eat or drink—if he does I do not notice, so flawless is his art. For he is an artist; a well-greased automaton could not outshine him. The mouth opens and closes over the words so efficiently! But—*what was that?* Something has happened. Something has gone wrong. Maurice continues to talk, but everything has changed!

I pay close attention to the old man's face. Perhaps he notices the difference in my look, for all at once his pale blue eyes look into mine and for the first time in our long history of evenings together, I fear that *he has seen me,* and is afraid that *I have seen him.* But, just what *is* it I have seen? I am gripped in the fist of an execrable panic and the pool that was so calm within me is stewing with those unnameable horrors that keep me awake. It costs me a tremendous effort to keep myself from striking Maurice and tearing from the room. For one mad moment I fear that the old man is after my life. That a trap has been set. That

Maurice is the spider and I the fly.

Maurice stops talking. He looks at me curiously. It is obvious that he has caught a glimpse of the upheaval going on within me. I stare at his face and wait. For it to happen again. And it does: suddenly his paralyzed hand is wrested by a violent spasm and twisted into a claw that swells hideously with blood. The spasm over, the hand rests immobile once again in Maurice's lap, a pink poppet of flesh.

"You must excuse me," Maurice says in a voice no longer equal but into which has crept a note of pleading; "I have these spastic attacks more and more often and I cannot do anything to stop them. They are not painful," he adds, as if to reassure me. I try to smile, to shrug, to shake the whole thing off, but it is impossible.

"I-I- forgive me. I do not feel well," I manage to mutter. "I'll get my coat myself." Grabbing my coat in the hall, I run from the building and do not stop running until I notice that people are staring at me.

❋

Three weeks have passed and it has been impossible for me to sleep. I survive by paying visits to the park and watching the little children at play. I dare not get into a conversation with any of the old people for the slightest tic, the smallest tremor thrusts me into the blackest despair.

There is a little girl who comes to the park in the afternoon— a charming, quiet creature with pink skin and pale blue eyes. She plays alone with her doll and for hours I watch her dressing and undressing it, telling it stories. She is so occupied that she rarely seems to notice me. I have upon occasion smiled at her.

The Jade Planet

For weeks the planet had approached steadily and now it filled the sky—a great disk of jade with darker green markings, its poles stained vermilion, its face flecked with gold. Soon it would swallow both sun and moon, and darkness would embrace the world forever.

From the planet's first appearance changes had been wrought upon the surface of the Earth. Beneath its weight polar ice was spreading, rain fell with the consistency of mercury, clouds like ceilings and blankets pressed down gloomily, birds lay flattened eggs, and infants were born with oddly elongated heads.

This morning he noticed that a skin had formed in his cup of cold coffee. Inevitably the sea would develop such a skin, and the sky. Over the Earth a cataract was forming. He foresaw that probes sent to explore the Jade Planet would return to Earth as crushed and creased as trilobites; fish would grow projecting spurs from head and breast, and men—imitating pre-Cambrian mollusks—protective shells.

This morning shadows took on consistencies. . . .

Tonight, a bright shield, the Jade Planet hovered above the world. Immobile it hung, oblivious of orbits. For an instant he saw that plague stained those vermilion poles, but as always his fear succumbed to the exacerbation of desire, and safe within the warm hulk of his bed, his body glowing, he penetrated the luminescent orb again and again, tearing at its clouds with his teeth until her seas foamed with sperm and he slept.

＊

It was in winter when the dark green patterns of the pale green world began to spread and thicken, grouping together in tortuous runes. Within a few hours a vast text had inscribed itself across the planet's face.

The unintelligible message haunted him. He tried to escape and walked lonely and desperate hours in a city where the foul air clung to his skin and beard like a rancid oil.

He feared that the green alphabet concealed a demonic charm; to decipher would be to succumb to evil; to read would be to fall from grace. But at dawn when the sky lifted and he returned to a room bright in the first light of day, when the uncanny words had ceased to move and nestled comfortably in the troubled gelatin of his mind, he was reassured and understood that the words were keys; that the Jade Planet and its message were a precious gift.

Falling into a deep sleep, the runes stretched out before him—undulating feminine arms beckoning, promising, willing. And at that moment, in those arms, he read his own immortality.

However, nothing was clear; the planet's truth barely glimpsed as behind a slippery film of ice. Threats, enticements, entreaties—the elliptic answers blazed until the very air had grown so thick he had to chew before he could breathe. The runes, sharp as scythes, balanced above him precariously; shapes if not meanings penetrated his very core.

Then at last, when he feared the mystery would cost him his life, the web the words had woven within his skull parted. Fearless he came to a great precipice—the enigma's very rim—and there he stood, ready to take the magnificent leap into understanding. It was at that instant that the characters—now so dark as to appear black—lifted themselves from the planet's pale surface to float eellike in luminosity.

The runes wriggled, coupled, broke, and regrouped; before his astonished eyes the Jade Planet disintegrated. Immediately after, burning brighter than any emerald, it snapped back into focus, swelled and twinned—as with a quickening of the heart he recognized the elastic dance of chromosomes and understood that what he had carried within him these long months was not a planet at all, but a cell—immense, hungry, malevolent—now in eclosion.

What Happened in the New Country

We complained to the city officials about the smell.
They said that we had made the smell ourselves and
that therefore they could not do anything about it.

I took an airplane to the new country. The president met me
at the airport. He rode on the back of a large black beetle,
and his police, driving small motorized toilets, flanked him. All
week we visited the factories. There were seven hundred thousand running night and day. The hum was deafening. The president had some cold beef fat brought up. We used this to plug up
our ears. The workers in these factories wore electrified helmets.
They were soldered to their heads. When a worker needed food
he was given an electric shock, and when he asked for sleep he
was recharged electrically. The helmets were yellow and resembled beehives. They seemed to have been made of gold.
When the workers died, they were melted down in a centralized
factory called by code the diminishing zone, and poured into
little tins like butter, and labeled. Later I managed to read one of
these labels. It read LITTLE BLACK SAMBO'S BEST. That night at the
president's house we ate pancakes. They tasted strange, and the
president explained that they had been kept frozen for many centuries in gigantic aluminum freezers. However, he added that the
butter was fresh and that I myself had seen it being made.

The morning before I was scheduled to leave, two strangers in
uniform came to my room as I slept. They sewed me to the mat-
tress and painfully erased my face. When they were finished
they cut me free and sent me home on the bus. The trip home
took me over three hundred hours and was considerably more
expensive than I had been led to expect. My wife refuses to believe this story and insists that my face remains just as it was
before.

***

The Smallest Muttonbird Island

This happened long ago, long before Kate married the man from New Zealand and went to live on the smallest Muttonbird Island in Doughboy Bay. Looking at a blue-green map, I envy Kate's intimacy with Doubtful Sound and Dusky Sound and Te Waewae Bay. I should love to explore the Hunter's Hills, Haast Pass, and the Canterbury Plains. I wonder: does Kate, always a walker, hike up to the far edge of Farewell Spit? Has Kate gone swimming in Pegasus Bay? Dreaming over the map of South Island at the world's end, following the thin red roads like veins with my finger, I can smell the sea-sucked air and feel the wind nuzzle my skin. And as I moon over a crumpled stretch of coastline and listen to the mewling birds, I imagine the strong, manly hand of Kate's husband on my shoulder.

Because I could do with a man; I could use a strong man's hand. I've not seen Aidan, but I imagine him craggy, salty-tasting, and great in bed. Aidan is a painter and famous for the way he paints the sky. A critic once described his work as being infused with moonlight. Looking at that damned map I wish to hell I was Kate; Kate loving Aidan on the smallest Muttonbird Island.

In my book of maps, islands are scattered everywhere like fish scales across the turquoise oceans. Some are no more than coral rings circling lagoons, bird sanctuaries the size of ballrooms. I see islands that are military bases, really just airstrips. Some islands are shaped like tears. But it is New Zealand that seizes my imagination and South Island especially because I suppose Kate and Aidan go there when they need supplies or a change of air. And if Kate's life, about which I know close to nothing, makes me dream, it is because my own can be dreamed no longer. Looking at the map I would give everything for a life in places Kate may be sick to death of by now.

✳

Children, Kate and I were friends. I lived beside the grave-yard and she beside the woods. Her closest neighbor was Mrs. Greenaway, who lodged the feebleminded. We often saw them sitting stunned and quiet on Mrs. Greenaway's front porch. My closest neighbor was a priest. He prayed for their souls but not for their minds because, he joked, "The Devil's already got their minds."

My room overlooked the cemetery. It was sunny and peaceful. In summer the paths twinkled like brooks of milk. In the fall they were thickly bricked with gold leaves. All winter grackles quarreled among the tombstones. Beyond, low hills and copses dissolved into country roads, a chicken farm, a highway. Kate and I visited the farm; we admired the two-headed chicks suspended in alcohol and carried home double-yolked eggs. We walked the forbidden highway all the way to the gas station café where we savored the thick exhaust of trucks and like the logger in the song stirred our coffee with our thumbs. But the place we especially loved was in the woods behind Kate's house, a cluster of elms felled by lightning, a clutter of naked trunks sprawling like lovers shipwrecked in sleep. The dead trees were our treasure hunts; our highways to planets haunted with the moonmen of our minds. Even now I dream of trees carved into the painted likenesses of our games, the totems of childhood. Even now I recall a crystal gazebo and the smooth walls of a fictive corridor better than the room I slept in last night, the face of the man I slept with.

Kate had a sister who had once made six bombs. Her boyfriend left for Poughkeepsie at midnight with the bombs wrapped in blankets like puppies in the boot of his car. He planned to blow up a bank. On the highway five hours later a milkman discovered a crater the size of a ballroom. Kate told me about how her sister sat out all night on the back porch waiting for a demon lover. She was a Weatherman, but she believed in ghosts.

Sometimes Kate's sister followed us into the woods. She would straddle a dead tree with Edgar Poe and suck her thumb.

107

We'd pray to God she'd leave because it was impossible to have fun when she was around. Just when we would forget that she was there, she would startle us by imitating birdcalls.

One afternoon Kate and I lay on our backs in the woods beneath the sky watching wasps. They dropped from the air to drink dew from the throats of peculiar, furry flowers. And as insects sawed and ticked and the wind tugged at the highest branches, the day's games began to blossom in our minds. But then Kate's crazy sister was hooting after owls in the path, and Kate and I scrambling into the shadows to escape her, leaping off and away like startled jackrabbits. We flew across a tiny bridge we had never seen and descended into deeper, darker woodland, laughing like lunatics to have fooled her. We came to a ravine, a pathway worried ages ago by ice, and threaded on for close to an hour. We found some curious black and white feathers and pretended that the way was mapped by witches. The trees thinned out and soon the sun was burning in our hair. We had come to a meadow, an island of light framed in the rich, green fabric of the wood. It might have been the meeting place of fairies burnished by a thousand years of midnight dancing. It might have been the airstrip of celestial explorers. We stood in silence thrilled by the beauty of the place, not daring to move, afraid that one more step and the meadow would melt away. As we stood a woodpecker hammered the air and a doe bounded once around the clearing's rim. We waited, wondering what other magic the meadow had up its sleeve. We might have been creatures of ether contemplating Heaven, two featherless mut-tonbirds treading air. (For I have read that petrels—and mut-tonbirds are petrels—never touch the ground until the time has come for them to lay their eggs. They copulate in flight, which is, I think, the finest, the freest way to love.)

This sweet, still moment was pierced by the shrill complaint of a blue jay. Clattering through the forest, he alighted in the leaves beside us. And it was then, when turning away from the sunlight and prying the shadows after him with our eyes, that we saw her hunched very near us, half hidden in the trees.

"Your sister!" I whispered.

"A *hunter!*" In the shifting shadows it was impossible to tell just who or what it was.

Kate and I were wary of hunters and in hunting season when we tramped the woods on weekends we wore red and shouted at the top of our lungs: HUMAN BEINGS HERE!

"It's not hunting season."

"Probably just a lumpy old tree!" But somebody was there. The world cracking beneath our feet, we crept through the forest until we were close enough to see that the old woman who stood hunched over a thick stick, gazing out upon the meadow with a stupendously idiotic expression on her face, was one of Mrs. Greenaway's feebleminded pensioners. Her wide, white forehead, her chin like a shovel, her stoop were unmistakable. Kate and I had often spied on her as she sat rocking on Mrs. Greenaway's front porch along with the two other idiots she cared for: Dracula and Watermelon Head.

"It's Old Bogey!" Kate whispered too loudly. The hag's head pivoted and Kate and I were seized and plumed by a pair of exceedingly daft eyes, skewered through and through like little birds ready for fire.

"Hello, Mrs. Neely," Kate faltered, swallowing hard. She took my hand. Together we stood riveted to her face, a face like a lopsided moon, worried and pinched with age. When Mrs. Neely put forth a long and limber tongue and made it loll about her chin and cheeks we looked on helplessly. There was a sound like a far whistling wind—Mrs. Neely was breathing. Behind her head the meadow reeled, a venomous wheel spinning in the bosom of the wood. Mrs. Neely's tongue wagged and craned like the neck of a goose. It could have been an eel or a drugged snake flailing the raw air. When it rooted in one nostril and then the other, it could have been made of rubber. This Mrs. Neely was a bestiary, a grimoire of lewd things. We watched her do her trick, in and out, hither and thither, over and over again. Uttering a small, shrill piping, Kate grabbed my wrist. But I was bewitched. That tongue was a sickle, a noose, a hook. That tongue was a hellish map unrolled. I wondered how she did it. She must have been at it for years.

When Kate pinched my arm to break the spell she left a mark. Even now I feel it like a vaccination acting up in evil weather. We turned away and stumbled back through the dim wood towards home without once looking back. I ran certain that Mrs. Neely's extravagant tongue bounded after us. Once I felt it strike me and cried out. Kate screamed. We arrived home after dark.

That night when she went to her room, Kate saw that her sister had snared her sheets. Kate remade her bed and slept.

✳

Looking at a blue-green map, I imagine the smallest of the Muttonbird Islands, an island so small it has no features, no name. I'd like to think it is an island without shadows, a circle of enchantment free of devilry. I'd like to think that such a place exists, that somewhere there is a man like Aidan, a Muttonbird Island for me. But this cannot be. Because I am not worthy of happiness. You see, unlike Kate, I have let the hag into my heart.

Grace

When she was a small child, Lilly and Lola would braid her hair. The three of them would sit together in the scattered sun of the front porch, and the little twinnies' lisping whispers, the attentiveness with which they touched her hair, would send her into a state close to ecstasy. There would be a breeze like a warm breath, like the even, warm breathing of a sleeping kitten nestled against her exposed neck. And there would be birds scrabbling in the low berry bushes that wreathed the lawn, a puppy yelping in a pine-paneled room, the evening meal in preparation and so the tempting smells of cornbread and roast chicken wafting from her mother's kitchen or one of the neighbor's kitchens, the homes all built in a closely knit circle and facing a round plot of grass planted with one handsome evergreen, at Christmas foamed with snow and made precious with red and blue lights. In a near future she would sit under this tree after dark with a boy, kissing.

❋

Earlier that week Gracie had been invited to a birthday party. On a thick square of paper folded into four she discovered an image of seven dwarfs stirring something creamy clockwise in an immense baby blue and ivory bowl. The tiny men were equipped with cunning ladders, soft, peaked hats, and long, thick spoons. She knew she had been cheated when she went to the party and neither the dwarfs nor the bowl of enchanted custard was to be found anywhere.

❋

Lilly unbraids Gracie's hair; Lola brushes it out once again. She starts at the top of the head (the *crown*, Gracie thinks happily to herself) and pulls the brush down, down, down Gracie's long hair, down the back of her head, neck, shoulders, and spine. Gracie's nerves thrill. Small, circular patches of sunlight fall through the leaves and slide past the porch railing to her feet. A gentle breeze caresses her. It is as if the entire universe is kissing her everywhere.

❋

Lilly and Lola hover above Gracie's head; the air quivers with the wings of their whispers. Gracie imagines that she is the center of a miraculous clock of the sort one sees in museums, a figure of porcelain sitting beneath a glass bell; Lilly and Lola articulated mechanisms, their lispings petals scattered on the glass in gold paint that is flaking. And yet, she is very much alive. Beneath its smocking, Gracie's heart is flushed with pleasure.

❋

Gracie's eyelids are so heavy. She cannot keep them up. The sun reels past, one sparkling element of a fabulous mechanism. The smooth, sweet hours are the meshings of wee metal teeth, like the teeth of magic mice. A distant bell chimes. With each stroke a gold coin drops into Gracie's heart. Her heart is a great pot yawning at the end of a rainbow.

❋

Many years later, after her separation and nervous breakdown, Gracie, greying and worn, is given pills. As she sits in the shadows of the porch of the clinic, she holds two in her open hand. They taste sweet and bring to mind the candy pearls bakers use to decorate fancy birthday cakes. They numb the pain and engender sleep. They take her back in time to summer afternoons when the twinnies—Lilly and Lola—lisped and whispered over her, brushing and braiding her long golden hair.

The Genius

The summer of my tenth year, Father took me to the sea.
Our hotel was built by the shore; the fine, white sand crept
up through the cracks of the freshly waxed floors and settled in
minute piles behind the dining room curtains. Across the road
from the hotel lay the beach, unusually free of seaweed and
shells. There were only myriads of tiny worms that made
whorls in the sand like a murderer's magnified fingerprints,
shrimp which the girls and women caught in small nets, and
crabs. I was enchanted with the clean beach and its fine, mal-
leable sand, and set about at once with my shovel and bucket to
build a city. I called it Heaven City because it was so white. By
the end of the afternoon, Heaven City was of such singular design that when Father came to fetch me for super, he found me
surrounded by an enthusiastic crowd eager to inform him of
what he knew already: I was a gifted child.

I had built Heaven City very high upon the beach so that the
tides could not reach it; I could go back to it each day, repair
crumbling walls and add new structures. I allowed no other
child into the game, and if a certain party of American psy-
chologists had not been vacationing on the very same beach
and keeping a jealous eye on the city, the other children—envi-
ous of the attention I was getting and the large area I had mo-
nopolized—would have gladly kicked the whole thing in.

One morning when the city had been under construction for
over two weeks, I discovered that the outer wall (including several watchtowers and a bridge of which I was especially proud)
had been erased and replaced by other structures of far supe-
rior design. As the eminent Dr. Chorea and his group had been
keeping a constant watch over Heaven City (they were taking
notes for a film and Dr. Chorea himself was writing an article
about me for *Psychology and the Creative Child*), I was certain

that no child had altered my construction. In any case, the work was far too sophisticated to be that of a child. It seemed very likely that one of the members of Dr. Chorea's group was playing a joke on me and the eminent doctor. I was convinced of this the following day when I discovered that the orientation of the observatory had been changed and that three beautifully executed parapets had been added to the exterior wall. Heaven City was taking on a most extraordinary aspect—there was nothing like it in my cherished *Illustrated Encyclopedia of World Architecture* that I had brought with me for the summer. I had "met my master" and, not used to being humiliated, was angry. I decided, however, that I was not beaten.

All afternoon I destroyed my poorer efforts and replaced them as fantastically and imaginatively as I could. I worked feverishly and with inspiration until nightfall. Imagine my fury when the following morning everything had been wiped out and replaced by one elegant and magnificent fortress—complete with a complex system of roadways and defenses—surrounded by high sculptured walls and thirteen ominous watchtowers. Angry as I was, I was nevertheless impressed by these structures and rather than better them (which I could not do) or destroy them (which would have been criminal) I began a large castle to the left of Heaven City and into which I put all that I had left of ingenuity.

That afternoon, as was his habit, Dr. Chorea came to see Heaven City and, ignoring my latest and most accomplished attempts, enthusiastically admired the work of the unknown architect. Mortified, I said nothing, but acknowledged silently to myself that he was right—my latest efforts were trivial and childish compared to the other. I decided that very night I would discover my rival's identity.

At about two in the morning when everyone was fast asleep I left the hotel and crept down to the sea. Silently I approached Heaven City from behind a line of beach houses that cleaved the street from the shore. One of these belonged to my father and stood just behind my new castle, to the left of Heaven City. I slipped inside and, leaving the door slightly ajar, waited.

Perhaps I dozed a little, perhaps it was only a half sleep, but

114

at dawn something stirred in the sea and at once wide awake I saw a large crab scuttle to the shore. He was deep blue and green but for his thorax which was white, and whirred like the electric fan suspended above the hotel dining room.

He was covered with chalky barnacles and although one of his legs was missing he moved quickly across the sand. Without hesitating he scuffled directly to my new castle. For several moments he remained motionless but for his thorax which continued to flutter. And then suddenly, and with furious energy, he threw himself upon it and broke it to bits with his great green pincers. Then he scuttled back and forth across the sand until not a trace of the castle remained. Blood pounding in my ears, I watched as he entered Heaven City and built a divinely proportioned aqueduct, a sophisticated canal system, and five smooth tetrahedrons each over one foot high. Then he explored Heaven City (now but for six inches of outer wall entirely of his own invention), scrambled down the broad white avenues, up and down numerous stairs, under bridges and across parapets, and then, entirely satisfied, dug a hole in the facade of the observatory (which had so particularly excited Dr. Chorea), crept inside and disappeared.

Head spinning, I ran back to the hotel and upon reaching my room was sick on the carpet. However, next morning I went down to breakfast as usual. Dr. Chorea was sitting at our table with Father and was waiting for me. I had no choice but to sit down beside him. My father nodded and stirred his coffee; the doctor squeezed my hand. I could see the hair that garnished his nostrils and decided that I did not like him. Softly he told me that he had visited the beach that morning and that Heaven City was no longer there. Evidently the tides had been unusually high the night before—Heaven City had been washed away. He was pained—he had not even begun the film—he was distraught—his article was so promising—he was sorry. Taking my hand in his, he begged that I begin a new city; the film he was planning would be the crowning point of his career. He was convinced of my startling precocity—my *genius*.

The waiter had just then set a steaming plate of scrambled eggs before me. I threw this with all my force at the doctor's head and to my astonishment—severed it. Father raised his hand to strike me—something he had never done before—but changed his mind and reached instead for a cigar. Mechanically the waiter bent down to pick up the doctor's head as he might a deviled egg. Evading him, it scuttled sideways under a table. I insisted he catch it, which he did with the help of a long-handled serving fork. He presented it to me in a folded dinner napkin.

All the way to the beach the head squirmed, crablike, in its freshly laundered prison which smelled pleasantly of starch. (For a fleeting instant I thought of the doctor's impeccable shirts.) I came to the shore. The head now closely resembled a crab in volume and weight. With a cry I threw it with all my might out to sea.

When I returned to the dining room I saw that Dr. Chorea's body had been placed in a large crystal vase on the dining room mantel and that a beautiful bouquet of sea flowers was growing where his head had been. The gold buttons of the doctor's vest and jacket fizzed and sparkled in the water behind the crystal. A potted plant of sorts, Dr. Chorea was far more attractive than when he had been a man.

Theft

He took my head while I was sleeping. He kept it in vinegar for three days. Then he boiled it down and put it in an oversized eggcup. When he peeled it he was surprised to find that it still bled. Grinding his teeth, he set it to boil once more. An hour later he tested it with a meat fork. Satisfied that my head was done, he set it in a bowl and cracked it open with a silver mallet. Inside he found a thriving colony of red ants. Furious, he spat into my face and doused the skull with insecticide. Then he threw my head into the river and if a certain fisherman had not presented it to the proper authorities, I should never have found it again.

Lunch

The table is set. The children, their parents, grandparents, aunts, and uncles are all killing time on the lawn. The children are playing Skin the Cock; they have healthy red faces. Their parents are smiling, their teeth are good. Some of them are wearing glasses, others are chewing gum.

The women wear halters made of skin. The men wear rubber shoes and codpieces. The grandparents are sitting in oddly shaped wicker garden chairs.

Everyone is smiling. A few of the men are cracking jokes under the lilac tree. Jokes about defecation, the war, birth, and defecation. The lilac tree is in bloom, great purple grapes of the stuff hang loosely. The smell fills the air, settles in the ladies' armpits, handbags, the men's hair, the children's skin.

The dining room is cool, dark. A vast bouquet of lilacs fills the center of the table. The table is set, the cold dishes are waiting. The food is prepared in envelopes of skin, most of it is sealed in grease—the preference of the country.

The grandparents are eating small pink envelopes of ground meat fried in grease. From time to time they defecate into their chairs, which are really portable toilets made to look like simple wicker garden chairs. The sound of mastication, defecation, old people exchanging memories. The children are playing String the Frog on the lawn. They are stringing the frogs together with thin metal wire. Screams of delight, childish laughter. The frogs move spasmodically—the object is to see who can make the longest chorus line of dancing frogs.

The game of Skin the Cock has been over now for nearly two hours. The dead bird is being devoured by dogs in the courtyard behind the kitchen, the feathers are strewn all over the courtyard and the lawn. From time to time a gentle breeze lifts the feathers into the air. Some have settled in the lilac tree.

Shoes and Shit

Precocious at ten, Charlie Horowitz, my grandfather, a recent émigré to New York City from Omsk, ran away from home to join Mr. Barnum's Big Top. He changed his name to Harris, and his first money-making job in this life consisted of watering the elephants and sweeping up their shit.

✸

Grandpa suffers from emphysema.

"You would have appreciated the Fat Lady," he wheezes confidentially as he leads me by the hand to the Dairy Delight man who stands sweating and ringing his bell just across the street from the trim white house in Flushing, New York, wherein elephants proceed across the living room mantel with the slowness of stones.

"In those days the fat ladies were *really very fat!*" And as he pays for my ice cream: "Elephant shit ain't nearly as nasty as human shit." I smile up at him gratefully.

✸

A young man with a dream, Charlie Harris left the circus to shine shoes beneath the bright lights of Broadway. Alone in a spare rented room, he studied orthopedics and slowly worked his way to the top—his own shoe store in Miami. By the time he had retired he had tucked away a tidy sum, although not the million simoleans he had dreamed.

"A shoe has to be comfortable," Charlie pontificated. "Even a movie star ain't gorgeous if her feet hurt her."

✸

I liked Grandpa's Florida store. Fat ladies in florals crowded into Harris Shoes to sit feverishly fanning their breasts in the fourteen matching vinylite chairs Grandma had picked up in Daytona Beach *from a schwartz for a song.* Discreet, I looked on from a corner, hypnotized by the sounds of breathing and the sight of my promiscuous grandpa massaging martyred feet.

❋

The back room behind the store where Charlie and Francis Harris slept over nights when business was heavy—*Business is heavy, Dad; we'd better sleep over*—was decorated with framed testimonials from satisfied customers (not out front where the AMA could see them and *get wise*). One of these letters particularly impressed me. It said that my own grandpa was a saint. Which corroborated what my mother had always known: *Only a saint could live with Francis.* I wondered: *Could Jews be saints?*

❋

As we stroll back to that little white house in Flushing (this back when Charlie was still working for *that vampire in Hoboken* [Francis]) and a year before the move to Miami, and as my grandmother hysterically prepares a meal, Charlie Harris says this wonderful thing. He says:

"A man can't shit if his shoes don't fit."

Ms. Carolina Phipps

for Bin Ramke

Roderick Tuttle was a small man and very handsome; shy also and susceptible, prone to sleepless nights. He wrote fiction, excelled in the condensed and foreshortened. His small office was spare as well: white walls, the chosen books he read obsessively, the Greeks he taught and—what made his office singular—an extensive collection of large cacti.

Rod's greatest mistake, greater even than the brief affair he'd suffered with his brilliant, crazed cousin Amelia, was fathering "The Feminine Voice," a program conceived to bring "living women writers" to the campus for an evening's reading. It had been a mistake because the women were often very neurotic for some reason; sickly or alcoholic, sometimes drugged, always terrifically vulnerable it seemed and always vain; the reading their justification, or so he had come to see it, for being demanding, domineering, shrill, tearful.

They made passes at Roderick, especially the older ones who were often very much meatier than he; they alarmed him:

Agatha Dearling who had been brought in from Manitoba and who—after a disastrous reading during which she unaccountably kicked over the podium sending a pitcher of water onto the Provost's lap—had boozily confided that she'd not been laid in years. She had held Rod's hands so tightly his right index finger had never recovered; perhaps she'd aggravated arthritis he hadn't realized he had.

Lilith Turner, known for her book of fictions thirteen lines long and all treating occult themes. He had liked her stories very much, had even corresponded with her about them; Lilith had illustrated the slim volume herself with idiosyncratic figures of demons no bigger than postage stamps. She turned out

121

very unlike what her photograph had implied; she had an unusually broad posterior and incongruous arms like sticks and an odd way of poking her finger into Rod's ribs when she was speaking and into her own ear when he was. She had thrown herself at him in the parking lot of her hotel, the quaint and recently refurbished Pisenlit where all Rod's visitors were housed as the faculty wives offered their spare rooms no longer. He had lied to Lilith, told her that he was married; she had called him admirable; he had pecked her cheek with all the wistfulness he could muster and was relieved when Hi Short in Middle English offered to take her to the airport in the morning.

Gloria Novalis, the great beauty and his most daunting guest; Ms. Novalis despised all other women with such passionate vocation that she had burned one of Rod's favorite graduates—who had approached her with the intention of offering her a small sandwich—on the face with a cigarette.

✳

The semester had only just begun and already Rod was losing sleep; a reading was scheduled for the last Friday of September. He'd heard (too late) that Carolina Phtipps was a notorious man-hater, asthmatic, and a vegetarian who only ate grains. Ms. Phtipps was expensive; she traveled with a retinue: her giant schnauzer Pecker and Yukon Cleet—a woman who, from what he gathered, fulfilled the office of bodyguard. As it turned out, at the last minute Ms. Cleet was hospitalized with severe pesticide poisoning.

Friday came. Rod could not accustom himself to the idea that he was to pick up Ms. Phtipps, fearful of airplanes, and her schnauzer at the bus station in an hour. He tried to lose himself in the minor details her impending arrival demanded. He called the Pisenlit to remind them to install the humidifier. He called the Bird's Nest to be assured that a table for two (sadly Hi was unable to make it) would be waiting; the owner informed him that the evening's menu offered a dish containing no less than five kinds of rice and a *coulis* of spinach. Then Rod drove to the bookstore. The familiar black and green cover of *Pneumonia* was clearly visible, even from across the street.

The Lunatic's Apprentice

Was Florida, the monk, a lunatic? He argued that in the pebbles of the path he could read the destinies of pedestrians. That the night sky was alive with white flies in whose dizzy loops he could foresee debilitating fevers.

He bragged that he had invented a system for warding off beggars, lepers, demons, and small children; that he had written a celebrated treatise linking regional pronunciations of vowels to indigenous facial tics. He had once found an egg as large as a cow, and a cow no larger than an egg—and he had offered them both, along with his treatise, to the queen of Spain.

Was the monk insane?

Publius, the novice, was convinced he was a saint. He believed him when, refusing lunch, Florida explained that he fed upon stones and the fluid fog of evening.

"Do not forget, fellow servant," Florida liked to repeat, "I have no need of porridges, vegetables, and meat. Yea, I take my nourishment from the evening's glair and the dry lichen which —as you see there—clothes the naked cliff."

❋

Publius sold Florida's charms to the crones who hobbled about at the bottom of the hill. These broken bits torn from the backs of old books, of yellowed parchment and dust pilfered from the ossuaries of saints, brought relief to shriveled hearts and swollen feet and gave Florida the ready cash he needed to buy the sweets and pickled fish he secretly craved.

The monk was curiously erudite and never ceased to astonish his apprentice. He required Publius to shun the seductions of what he called "the sumptuous, tactile world," to flee, as plague, the pagan weddings of flowers, to deny his passionate love of old statuary (brother Basilides had recently unearthed some badly shattered marbles a stone's throw from the monastery); to distrust the inebriating raptures of language and yes, even Florida's own impassioned speeches (and this confused Publius); never to stare upon the glabrous skins of snakes; to run from boys, ewes, and young women and the forked silhouettes of olive trees at the edge of evening.

Other than that, Publius must do what he had always done: he must sweep and scrub and after meals, he must swab the table down. And one day he would learn to levitate, just as Florida did whenever he wished, and live on fog and fungus too.

To levitate! How the lowly scullion would love to leave the bitter earth to tread the lovely air! And what must he do to be worthy of such ecstasy?

Firstly: He must—each crepuscular dawn—scrape his tongue off with a stick.

Secondly: He must never bathe his body, but rub it clean with sand; rub it raw with sand, above all in the cracks.

Thirdly: Should he ever have to write anything down, anything at all, he must do it from right to left—else the words be intercepted by any of the multiple spirits of mischief which proliferate in the air worse than gnats, moths, butterflies, wasps, horseflies, birds, bats, sand fleas, flying fish—*flying fish?* And—don't interrupt—mosquitoes. For like the dust they are numberless and invisible, invisible and numberless—

"*¡Cielo Santo!*"

Florida taught his apprentice that upon the piebald pelts of cats can be read the Devil's coded messages. He would one day show him the imp he owned who angrily gesticulated in an unbreakable glass bottle. Florida could conjure up a swarm of frogs for Publius should he wish it, but the apprentice feared frogs and begged him not to.

✳

When with the others the apprentice gathered simples on the hill, he turned his head away from the rude protuberances of stone everywhere in evidence. Florida had warned him that projections of any sort were as dangerous as cracks and craters. As long as Publius dealt in bowls and cups and spoons and the manipulation of nodular vegetables, he could not hope to fly. (Florida not only levitated, he flew—he had visited the sun, the moon, and more than once perceived the giddy gates of Heaven.)

After he had scoured the old oak table and his own self, Publius went into the chapel and stood above the black marble basin of holy water. And in that breathing mirror, he saw reflected his own face. It was an honest face, kind, shallow-pated, and mild. That night, having supped upon nothing more than a bowl of hot water embittered with weeds, he attempted to rise into the air. But the effort frightened him, as it occurred to him that, should he succeed, he might never again return to earth.

In the middle of the night, fierce growls awoke him, as if— he told Florida the next day—wild beasts had been prowling beneath his ribs. Darkly, Florida hinted at something worse than beasts.

"But not . . . *demons!*" Publius paled. Had he felt their beaks and bristles? He had.

"You must always listen very intently." Florida was cross. "These rumbles are among the more esoteric aspects of the languages of darkness which I am attempting to decipher. Demons are more voluble than pretentious scholars and their parrots. The intestinal gasses are ignited by their burning blasphemies. There are more devils in your earwax," he continued to Publius's humiliation, "than there are teeth in all the head bones of humanity, present, past, and future."

Publius decided to stop eating altogether and to never again speak of his physical self, to—by means of virtuous self-government—convince Florida that to achieve grace he was ready to undergo any trials: to starve, to destroy his eyes in the translation of the obscure affirmations of ants, and—should Florida insist—suffer the clammy company of frogs. He knew that to partake of Christ's flesh was not to sin nor to cheat, but he feared that his lusting after that nearly immaterial crust every hour of the day, every day of the week, was.

The monks all shared a singular aptitude for distilling the sweet juices of the berries and simples that grew on the hill in profusion. With patience and science, they created greatly appreciated medicinal gums. Florida alone did not participate in this activity which he abhorred. The devils incarnated in the berries and herbs were not dissolved by the process (as a smirking brother Basilides suggested) but on the contrary increased a thousandfold. The others did their very best not to succumb to exasperation even when Florida bleatingly accused them of alchemy, hydromancy, and sedition. It had occurred to him that his fellow monks were poisoning the people of Spain. That their gums precipitated plagues, convulsions, and delirium. That the monks were Jews. (Was not alchemy rooted in the esoteric traditions of the Semites? And did not the Semites worship Belphagor who dwelt among rocks? And Beelzebub the fly? And did his brain not buzz all night long and in the daytime too?)

Florida wrote—from right to left—a letter describing his worst fears and addressed it to the Inquisitor General and his Council Supreme:

As the sun rose I read in the Zodiac's fading glossaries the intent of our own fulgent destinies—we must destroy the monks, their athanors and crucibles. . . . Our task is gigantic; not only must we fight our enemies and the escalating archons of the air, but especially our own so-called *better judgment*. We must be prodded onward, my Elect, not by our hearts and minds, but by the Blind Truth as it is revealed to us in the stars. We will scour the world of sedition until all is as white as boiled bones: the pelts of tigers, the petals of red roses, the black bodies of Africans and ants. . . .

Publius, to whom Florida confided, marveled and wondered how this heavenly laundering of the planet could be achieved. Florida explained that the natural world was a veil behind which imponderable and divine agents stir and act. One tiny thread pulled free and on earth all would be as in Heaven—flooded with white light.

Publius was troubled. He continued his duties in the kitchen and all the while wondered that the gently ironical brother

Basilides and the others, who seemed as good as lambs, were in fact sorcerers. He knew them well and loved them all. He had sucked the gums and never once been taken ill. The apprentice feared that his master, the brilliant Florida, who took his weekly walk upon the surface of the moon, who scoured his flesh with the sands of the sun, was very wrong.

✳

Florida grew increasingly crabby and morose. His letter to the Inquisitor General had gone unanswered. He was losing his authority. The apprentice, that half-baked scullion whose brain was no bigger than a button and who smiled when he was scolded, was deciphering with felicity, and alone, the bubbles in dishwater and the grimoires that wormed across the doors of ancient kitchen cabinets. He also dreamed profusely—gorgeous, deeply hued visions the likes of which Florida, who never dreamed, had never seen. For example: Publius dreamed of horns soaring like rockets across the scarlet sky excreting lexicons of holy fire. He dreamed of whispering shadows; they introduced him to Platonic philosophy.

And now the apprentice had the cheek to council his master in what he called his *own* mysteries; he babbled on and on about imbecile geometries explained to him by honeybees who, "swarming ever swelling out and inward drawing," taught him how to free his mind from ideas three-dimensional and to escape the sluggish elements by meditating upon the mutual congress of puissant, waxy hexagons.

And then it happened. Publius ascended into the sky. He floated in the sappy air above the monastery with the ease of a fish in water. He called upon his master to join him, but Florida could not, nor for that matter ever could. Heaven help him, he had lied. He had never learned to fly.

The others, harvesting berries on the hill, fell to the ground and prayed, but for brother Basilides who raised his arms to the heavens and cheered.

Consumed with jealous rage, Florida scolded Publius for his vanity, his presumption, his folly, his shameless impudicity—

for the apprentice's skirts did billow in the wind.

But Publius did not hear him. Chanting the esoteric geometries of bees and dreams, he soared ever higher into the air. His voice was a shrill, sugared piping and it was accompanied by a trilling of birds and a deep, melodious thrumming of insects.

One by one the others felt themselves shed gravity, and in exhilaration and hilarity Basilides and his brothers were lifted, soul by air supported, air from ether hanging. Their robes billowing and snapping, they flew away after Publius towards a horizon so achingly blue it rent Florida's heart, he wanted it so badly.

All that night and the next and the next, Florida lay upon the ground like the worm Adam was before the gift of breath, cursing the cosmos. And this is how the officers of the Inquisition, led up the hill by a centenary crone, found him.

I will Never Forget You Ernie Frigmaster

I deal in fancy footwear. My specialty is bedroom slippers for women. I carry all your latest styles: Marie Antoinettes, Lucretia Borgias, Joan Crawfords, and Jayne Mansfields, in the finest man-made fibers money can buy. I got your best brands too for example your Bickle's Angel Air Cushion. I own a nice modern store number thirty-four Olympus Lapis Lazuli Street Golden Years Florida to be exact. You have my address come on down any time and I'll be pleased to do business with you. You'll like the store I had it redecorated three years ago and it looks good by Charlie S. Clamhand of Clamhand and Sinke of Miami and it cost me over two thousand dollars and that ain't chicken crap. But Charlie gave me my money's worth I ain't grouching. Figged out a new window with fancy Spanish arches and a classy display of fine atticated prints of foot disease in full color very nice being as they is hand-touched with verible fourteen carats. But the *peas de Ritz* is a perfect skeleton of a foot and would you believe it this foot belonged to Bubbles O'Hara of silent screen fame and Charlie picked it up at an auction in Hollywood (California) in '52 as a curio never knowing he'd one day do over a store specializing in woman's fancy but figuring you never know. So I got it in the store on display on a velvet cushion between a picture of Bubbles O'Hara and an atticated daggertype of Cindyella trying on the glass sneaker. It goes over real big with the clients especially the elderly who remember seeing Bubbles cakewalking in her heyday and the novelty don't wear off. Lots of times my customers bring in relatives just so's they can steal a look at Bubbles's soup bones and I sell a lot of merchandise this way.

Now I knows what you're thinking. You're thinking what with all these classy prints and a skeleton in the store there must be more to me than meets the eye and you ain't whistling

"Dixie." Lots of folks come in thinking I must be one of your foot-type doctors. Well I ain't no *certified* doctor but I'll tell you a secret. I got these *magic hands.* Now don't go asking me how or why 'cause I don't rightly know myself. But they is magic and I can cure sick feet with them. I don't advertise—don't want to get the AMA down my back. But when people what's suffering come into the store and see Charlie's poshy knick-knacks they get the idea I must be some sort of a doctor and they ask for help. Well I says I ain't one of your *certified* doctors but sure as rain I can fix sick feet. And I can. I have a testiment from Mrs. Quincy Clorke of Alberta Canada to prove it. A nice-looking woman but big weighing over 250 pounds. She comes into the store wearing a pair of godknowswhat size twelve extra wide. Feet so swollen they's sloshin' out over the tops. She sees Bubbles's remainders and asks if I am a doctor. I say I ain't *certified* and explain about the magic hands. She says help me doctor I won't be ungrateful. So I take her to the back of the store and I tell her to sit down and take off her shoes. I kneel down and take hold of her feet. They is hotter 'n hell. I start strokin' and pattin' and rubbin' up and down and over the tops and under and around the back. Pretty soon she closes her eyes and starts moanin' and rockin' back and forth so's I can see she likes it. I rub harder but I'm not rough with her see. I'm gentle. She moans again and the feet start feeling nice not so hot but the rest of her is getting hot! I tell her not to bother about me to make herself comfortable an' take off her dress so she does. She takes it all off. Let me tell you that Mrs. Quincy Clork of Alberta Canada is built to last. A lovely lady breasts like cucumbers. Tells me her name is Victoria. Tells me to rub her all over not just her feet so I do and we're both having a nice time. I make her happy and I feel that's part of being a good doctor not just making the sick part happy *but the whole person happy.* I liked Mrs. Clork and I made her up special a pair of Bickle's Angels with padded air vents. When she got back to Alberta she wrote me this testiment. I had it framed and it's hanging in the back of the store and not out front where the AMA can see it and get ideas.

Dear Mr. Frigmaster,

When I came into your store Friday July tenth 1964 I was not a happy woman. As you may recall my feet were sore I was in pain. Twenty-five years I suffered. But God has Mercy and His Arrow pointed the way to your store. You touched me with your Magic hands and for the first time in twenty-five years the pain stopped. I am a new woman. Even my husband Mr. Quincy Clork tells me. May Jesus be with you always. I am thankful for the day He led me to your store and I pray to Him each night that He will watch over you. In my dreams I feel the touch of your Blessed Hands.

Yours Sincerely,

Victoria Clork

P.S. I will never forget you Ernie Frigmaster.

Easter Melodies

Old Piano Legs

My mother's mother had a large glazed porcelain Pierrot. He wore a black skullcap and held a bunch of balloons. She was very proud of him. Perhaps the Pierrot was a lamp because in my memory he stands tall and bright in a low, dim room. If so, I can't remember if he had a shade, although I remember that my mother's blackamoor did. Was he near a window? I don't recall any windows. Everything else in that house is a smear, like words robbed of recognition with a filthy eraser.

I seem to recollect that Grandma's furniture was overstuffed, tasselated, and squat—just like Grandma who, even as a young girl, was called "old piano legs." In memory her rooms are dark and spotty like spoiled photographic plates—except for the Pierrot, his jelly-bean bright balloons, and, curiously, a bowl of clear soup with slices of carrot floating in it. I know I slept in her house but have no memory of the room. I have only a troubled impression of dimness, of murky halls and chambers enlivened by carrots burning like August moons, one Pierrot's pearly face and the blazing torch of his balloons.

This was Flushing, New York, in the spring of 1950. I arrived wearing a new bird's-egg blue coat and carrying a little straw handbag with sticky-looking cherries stapled to the top. Both were gifts from Grandma.

A girl was brought in from across the street to entertain me. The games she instigated in that featureless place increased the ambient opacity. She was nearly twice my age and sexually curious. I think that after she held me too tightly and called me "darling," I must have managed to convey something of my confusion to Grandma. Because after one kiss she fades away. I am left alone with the beaming Pierrot.

132

Eggs and Chickens

I vaguely recall an Easter cake that quite enchanted me although my mother bristled with disapproval when Grandma brought it to the table. There were yellow marshmallow chickens stuck in the frosting. Yet, beside those lambent carrots and balloons, they, like everything else, flicker and die.

My father also owned an interesting object. It was a bottle shaped like a skeleton sitting on a barrel of whiskey. Six cups went with it: porcelain skulls not much bigger than thimbles. Years later I saw the skulls of lemurs in a museum. They were very like those cups.

My mother had a weakness for blackamoors; she thought they were chic. A disturbing lapsus for a Democrat. She never did find one for the lawn. But she did find a living room lamp at Perlmutter's: a black person in livery eighteen inches high with a fuchsia lampshade screwed to his turban.

Back to Easter. Another relic of my childhood worth mentioning is a sugar egg with a small cellophane window. Behind the window is a paper garden with hens and chicks walking around in it. Despite the fact that we lived across the street from a chicken farm and I saw hens and chicks every day of my life, I spent hours with my eyes glued to that window. I was certain that if I could only make myself small enough to climb in and join those ideal chickens on the stenciled grass, I could be deliriously happy.

Clam Chowder

I remember a second bowl of soup. This is on Block Island and the soup is clam chowder.

In the summer of 1950, I spent ten days with Grandma. Our hotel was perched on a promontory of rock overlooking the Atlantic. I had with me two identical yellow dresses. They were Easter gifts and had cherries embroidered on the pockets.

Grandma became acquainted with a young man in the hotel supper room. He gave me his soup crackers. One afternoon he joined us for a walk along the beach. The ocean was very rough and although it was too dangerous to swim, many delicious, shallow pools of fresh seawater had formed beneath the cliffs. Grandma told me to take off my dress and bathe. I was shy but she insisted and I had not yet learned how to resist anyone.

As Grandma held my dress folded neatly over her arm, I crept into the pool and, kneeling, pretended to ignore them both. I scooped up seaweed and lay it, sopping wet and streaming, in garlands of green and purple at my throat. I know I looked innocent enough, yet I was actively seducing the stranger. And if—other than his very black hair and pale face—I have no memory of what he looked like, if marshmallow chickens have left a far greater impression, I will never forget the tender heat with which his eyes played upon my body; my feeling of shame. My feeling of power.

F*a*ı*ʀ*y F*ı*n*ɢ*e*ʀ

for Harry Mathews

Not many days before her ninth birthday, scrubbing herself in the bath with a natural sea-sponge that looked like the ear of an elephant, she discovered a part of herself tucked away like a pearl button or the tender, firm bud of a rose. Gently caressed with the sponge or, better still, her own middle finger, it gave her intense pleasure. The spasms were so violent that for one crazy moment she thought that she had been hurtled out to sea, her salty bath bewitched, whipped to a froth by the cyclone that circumvoluted her spine. Transmuted from docile to wacky, given to sudden fits of mad laughter and hot tears, she retired early to bed where one half-hour later her father when looking in would find her blasted, in deepest slumber, grounded as if by lightning. He would return to the downstairs living room on tiptoe and perplexed. It did not occur to him that his daughter had discovered ecstasy.

❋

Everything excited her. She poured over her fairy books ignited by the baroque figures of evil witches leaning upon thick rods, windmills grinding pearls and roses into dew, bowlegged elves with long, softly turgid hats and spinning saucer eyes, and lean, hard princes steadily advancing through underbrush and bramble.

❋

Oddly enough, she had not believed in fairies until now. Burnished by her fire, the figments of her daydreams grew solid

---

135

and featured. Their laughter roused her in the middle of the night and in half-dream she saw them cavorting in the dark: little Ned Needle wee, magic Manroot, the tiny twins Ram and Goldenrod—polishing shoes and sewing on buttons, buttons of pearl like rosy drops of dew, shining like the eyes of a stallion steadily advancing, whinnying, now trotting, quickening, now charging, his head straddled by two strong princely legs, his nostrils flaring, breathing fire, body steaming, mouth foaming: *dragon-horse, dragonfly, horsefly, deer-fly*, buzzing, stinging, ringing—and coming she cries out, her pillow transformed to the stallion's straining, sweating back, carried away by the Prince of Fire himself, her own master Elf-of-Ten; she names him: F*a*i*r*y F*i*n*g*e*r.

Janie

Amnesia is viewing Dr. Moebius's holograms. After much hesitation (and Amnesia is charming when she hesitates) she chooses a blue horn.

Dr. Moebius commends her good taste. However, horns are far more difficult to seed than scales, or gills. The simplest procedure at this stage (and the least expensive) is a sex change. But no, Amnesia wants her daughter *horned*.

Of course she realizes that the baby will have to be delivered by cesarean section? Amnesia nods eagerly. The doctor tells her that in nature, blue is rare. He does not tell her that the sky itself is not truly blue. Long before Amnesia was born the sky turned orange.

The only animal he can think of that produces blue pigment is a bird of the family of *Musophagidæ*. He has seen a single irritable couple at the Algiers zoo. Curiously enough, the bird's pigmentation washes off in the rain. He laughs, swaddling Amnesia in a cloud scented of rubber.

Amnesia frowns. Dr. Moebius assures her that the baby's horn—its cells puffed with air and resting on a membrane of genetically induced melanophores—will be colorfast. He guarantees that in expectation of special occasions, his blue horn takes on a metallic shimmer and casts a purple shadow. Amnesia sees extinct dragonflies hovering above an unearthly mud that slides out from under the doctor's desk.

※

It is rumored in Amnesia's tarot circle (although she is unaccountably shy and dares not ask) that a daughter's private parts can be made to scintillate. Like her best friend, Anaesthesia, Amnesia wants her daughter to be the most perfectly desirable

137

creature on the planet and when the time comes, the favorite of a most uncommon man, a powerful man with the fixedness of purpose of a hungry snake.

Hummingbirds, elegantly copulating in the grumous penumbra of the office, give Amnesia the courage she needs to express her secret wish. The doctor shows no surprise, only chides her gently, reminding her that her daughter is a fetus not yet two months old. If the time is right to speak of horns, it is far too early to speak of love.

Amnesia blushes. Decidedly, she is utterly charming. Dr. Moebius, who cannot bear to see a young woman ill at ease in his darkened rooms, assures her that at puberty he will alter her daughter's hormones so that the brain will produce guanine—the stuff that makes fish shine.

Like moonbeams, mutable fish dart across the room. Amnesia is enchanted. Until now she has only seen her fish skinned and particled for fast-frozen sushi.

"The clitoral-rainbow effect," the doctor pursues as a full-grown trout leaps from his mouth, "is still under investigation. This memo from the lab suggests that a breakthrough is expected momentarily." As the message beeps and shuffles across his parted thighs, he concludes that the procedure will be faultless long before her daughter's twelfth birthday.

"Have you chosen a name for the driblet yet?"

"Janie!" Amnesia's smile is phosphorescent.

"An unusual name," approves Dr. Moebius. He pats Amnesia's knee in an irreproachable gesture of tender complicity.

Sleeping Beauty

It is written in the Sacred Books: at puberty she will be pricked and bleed and sleep one hundred years. Then a frog will tumble down the chimney and, leaving a rope of slime across the counterpane, kiss her. Or, depending on this and that, a wolf reeking of the shit of slain deer will leap into her bed and eat her. Beauty's destiny hangs from the fitful runes that totter and dance upon the face of the moon.

Not that she has read the books: *all* alphabets are denied her. Besides, her feet are so tightly bound that, had she been literate, she could never have crossed the square that severs her from the library.

Unfair! Isn't she a princess? If only her mother were here to explain! But Beauty's mother is dead—stoned for a fault with the cobbler, her bones ground into flour and baked into cake for the King.

She asks her Keeper: *Why?* The insufficient answer: *An old curse.* Long ago a woman, her name forgotten, had eaten an apple although it was forbidden. Ever since each female of the line must pay for the crime. *How?* Oh, that. . . . She will take a basket to her grandmother in the tower. And Grandmother will pull a pin from her breast and stab her. Beauty will shriek and fall to the floor as dead as a crystal ball. *What's in the basket?* Curds. Whey. New shoes, ruby red. Can she doubt it? This is the same grandmother who bound her feet.

❋

Puberty seizes Beauty. Parts of her body, hitherto anonymous, clamor to be named. Her blood smells metallic, of the forests she had glimpsed when once she had been carried to the thirteenth parapet in fever.

Beauty stares at the King's unintelligible calendar, its glyphs waxing day by day. She suspects an accord between numbers, the moon, and her destiny. She who had not been taught to count knows there is very little time.

That night as her Keeper dreams of tearing out the voices of crickets, Beauty sits beside the hearth's dead ashes and unbinds her feet. The toes have shriveled to the size of pearls. She reaches into the basket and, taking up the little shoes, slips them on. They are a perfect fit. And she remembers how, when once she had tottered beside her Keeper in the snow, she had left the smallest prints imaginable, and how the cobbler, looking at her lovingly, had measured them.

Already she is dancing. The throbbing shoes, red as hearts, give her wings. Beneath the moon, Beauty flies out the window, over the square, past the library, and beyond the high tower where a hag and a king, a frog and a wolf, sit together speaking of dark things.

Abracadabra

When he was a small child, he often heard buzzing in his ears, reminding him of bees, and he would simultaneously feel a sting in his throat which would make swallowing painful. Sometimes the buzzing rose to a high, piercing ring—like the hall phone only shriller and continuous—and he came to realize that extraterrestrial beings were listening to his most private thoughts. This flattered him, but it also frightened him. He knew that his thoughts were unique and that they were dangerous. His mother had often threatened him with punishment because she knew what he was thinking and it wasn't nice.

One day she caught him looking at himself in the mirror. She told him to stop at once because *the Devil will look right back at you.* From that moment on he could not stop himself from peering into mirrors or any reflecting surface and making faces. He managed to frighten himself although he had only wanted to show the Devil he *knew and didn't care.* But he soon discovered that it was not the Devil he saw reflected in the glass, but one of *them*—an extraterrestrial. It had somehow managed to take on his form—that of a seven-year-old boy with hair so pale it was almost white.

He made up a charm to confound it whenever he passed a mirror. He crossed his eyes and farted and frowned and showed his teeth. But it could see through walls and so in any house or place where there were mirrors he was not safe. He frowned and showed his teeth continually, crossed his eyes when no one was looking, and farted in corners when no one was near.

It could make itself very thin—as thin as a hair—in fact it could lie flat on his father's head disguised as a hair, or in straight shadows of staircases. It liked staircases best because it liked parallel lines. On any large staircase many of them could hide together. Staircases and sidewalk cracks; beneath radiators and between pages of books. But it hated the number three because three plus three is six and he was seven. It could not catch him on three. *Can'tcatchmeonthree!* It was simple. All he had to do was climb every third stair and fart when he came to a radiator. He blew into his books and poured salt into the bindings—they hated salt. It made them shrivel and die.

He was afraid to let them get hold of anything that belonged to him. Every time he urinated he spat into the toilet; he also put spittle into his ears to keep them from stealing the wax there while he was sleeping. They needed this wax in some mysterious way for their space vehicles. It was collected by large bumblebees and the space vehicles themselves looked very much like hives.

One day he was looking through his baby books. His mother had told him to clean up his room and to weed out his old things so that she could throw them away. He found his very first book—a large, cloth ABC. *A* was an apple (or pretended to be). But it was so red he could tell it was not an apple at all but instead a giant ruby, as big as a light or a signal—like those belonging to space vehicles. When he turned the page he came to the letter *B* and screamed. It was a picture of a bumblebee as big as his father's fist. Its stinger pointed at him menacingly. He had no choice but to defecate upon this image immediately. When his mother discovered what he had done, he was severely beaten.

❋

After the beating he was very tired. His body was red and hot and his mother tucked him into bed: *Don't make Mommy mad at you again!* His buttocks were very sore and he was afraid that should he ever defecate again he would most certainly die. Especially in a room with a mirror. The safest place would be the backyard. The dog did it there and the extraterrestrials would not know that his shit was his own. They would think that his shit was the dog's shit. From that time on, whenever he thought about it he would laugh.

He had always felt safe in his room. But after the beating

he was no longer sure. He spat along the four walls and under the bed. Then he noticed the doorknob on the door to his room. Not only did it reflect his image—it distorted it. For the first time he knew what the extraterrestrials really looked like. In panic he painted the knob over with red nail polish. Immediately he realized his mistake. The doorknob looked like the apple in the ABC.

The house was empty; his parents had gone out and had told him to stay in his room. But the red doorknob, bubbling malevolently, heated the room like a furnace. He realized that all this heat was being pumped into his room directly from the sun. If he stayed there he would be baked alive.

He decided to go out and sit in the hall where he would be relatively safe (there were no mirrors). But in order to leave his room, he'd have to open the door. For a moment he was paralyzed. But he had no choice. He would have to make a dash for it. He wrapped his hand in a sock so that he would not have to touch the doorknob which he knew was burning hot. Howling, he ran to the door. It was locked.

He stepped back in terror. He was locked in his room and they—they were in the hall doing terrible things to the dog. He could hear the dog scraping and whimpering at his door, trying to escape them. When the dog cried in pain he knew that they had used its body in some mysterious way. They needed the dog's excrement to get at him. The dog's shit was his shit. If they had the dog, they had him. There was only one thing left for him to do.

He went into his bed and wrapped the sheets and blankets around himself like a cocoon. He lay there with his hands over his ears and his teeth clenched and his eyes screwed shut so that he could not be entered by them in any way. Magically the sheets and blankets transformed to metal. The buzzing in his ears and the beating of his blood grew steadily in intensity until they were but one sound. And this sound came not from them, but from within himself. It was the continuous thrumming of a great motor, the motor of a swift ship entering into outer space.

When the key to the door of his room turned in the lock, he was already light years away.

The Folding Bed

The thought of murder was nowhere in my mind until she mentioned the folding bed. The folding bed on wheels that was so practical. She just shut it up with everything inside. It was the precise description of the bed that was so practical, its fusty sheets, burred goose-down pillow, and corrugated blanket all crammed together and wheeled into a dark corner of the second-floor landing, that did it. (I can still see the staircase. The varnish had been put on during a damp spell and had never dried. The dreadful staircase had smelled of dead horse feet for fifty years, years as discouraging as her backside. How I hated her, the staircase, and above all—that foul bed!)

"The sheets are clean!" she honked. "They've only been used three times and always by Uncle Walter." I considered the soggy rope of years that had unwound between the times the old salt had slept in the bed after relieving himself of his vague, goosey fantasies. I worked them out from the thumbed letters she kept in her dresser: 1941, 1948, and lastly 1957. And now a full eleven years later she was offering the bed to me. (Walter died back in 1958, six months after using it. His old man's stable smell still marked the bed like a neolithic handprint pressed to the wall of a damp cave.)

She took me upstairs. I noticed that her feet left soft, mossy maps on the sticky stairs. The higher we went the stronger was the smell of cigar corpses floating in stale beer. We reached the landing and I saw the bed lurking in the corner. Chatting all the while she rolled it out. The sight of those four black rubber wheels further enraged me. With difficulty she unfolded the bed, smoothed out the sheets, and turned to me, her eyes moist with pride and perhaps the memory of that bastard Walter. That wet look was the last straw and I immediately murdered her, all the while staring down at her aluminum dental plate. Before I left I took care to tuck her into the bed and to fold it up again.

Minus Twitty at Beetle Gulch

for Robert Coover

M inus Twitty rides into town raising dirt. His unwashed rear end rides high above a tooled belt that does not belong to him. If the naked truth be known, Minus Twitty has shot a taller man in Silver City in the back. He's been swimming in the dead man's saddle ever since.

Twitty figures Beetle Gulch is as good a place as any for laying low. The barber is willing to scrape the bristle from his cheeks and scrub the cooties from his head. With the cadaver's hard-earned cash, Twitty pays him for his talents, such as they are. Then he gets himself a room above the empty saloon. After dinner he retires to bed, and because there's nothing else to do, picks his teeth with a splinter he's pried from the floor.

The days and nights in Beetle Gulch are as unlively as eternity. There is no news of the murder, no news of any sort. Twitty plans to say his name is Randy should someone ask, and that his work is fancy horseship. Twitty means horsemanship, of course; however, no one asks. The townfolk's conversation— if punctuated by the sound of spittle slamming into polished spittoons—is as dry as the gulch itself.

Twitty stuffs the toes of the dead man's boots with his own randy underwear and hobbles down the street to look at the gulch again. There's nothing to see but a relic river as dry as a mummy's twat. Twitty thinks it's damned unfair that, now that he can afford one, there's not one woman to be had. Even the cook down at the saloon is a man and Twitty, say what you will, is not a sexual deviant.

After mulling it over all day he asks:

"Hey, Cookie—ain't no wimmen these here parts?"

"Nup."

145

"No wimmen!"

"Barber got 'un."

"Hum!"

"Yep!" The cook lards the spittoon.

"Where she at?"

"Keeps to bed."

"How she look?"

"Purty bad. Yessiree!" He swabs down the floor with a filthy mop. Gloomy, Minus sinks down deeper into his boots. But suddenly the other man stops swabbing.

"Hey! Hey!" he shouts, slapping himself furiously on the head. "Hey! I plumb firgot! There is warn!" Suddenly the cook has so much to say that the muddled Twitty asks him to repeat everything twice. There is a woman at the edge of town, young and pretty. Like Twitty, she's left a man behind in Silver City. She lives alone with her baby.

＊

Minus Twitty rearranges the wadding in his boots. He adds another hole to his belt with a rusty nail. Then he limps over to the woman's house, just to reconnoiter. His limited vocabulary makes no allowance for spooning. In plain English, Twitty plans to rape her.

The woman's shack of rotting wood crouches at the far end of the gulch. It does not occur to Twitty—who can handle only one thing at a time—that in this parched country there is something sinister, perhaps, about a hovel that exudes so much humidity. Despite the scorching sun, the place is steeped in fog. He does not see the hundreds of thousands of licorice-bodied necrophores who, with eager eyes, gaze up at him from their swarming buggeries.

After midnight, Twitty totters forth. And in the moonlight stumbles twice. When, breathing hard, he reaches the tiny house, he cuts the oiled paper window from its frame. Within, the woman sits up in bed. She says:

"Slide?"

The window is very much higher from the floor than he expects. Twitty tumbles in and, sprawling, loses a boot and scrapes a shin. As he scrambles towards the voice, he leaves a trail of socks. When he and the woman collide, she lets out a yelp of surprise.

"You're *not* Slide!"

Twitty slaps her face and grabs her. Caterwauling, she leaves a blue welt above his eye. With one hairy fist, he captures both her wrists. Together they collapse upon the floor, he panting, she mewling. He feels her writhing beneath his body. When she tries to bite his neck he slams his forehead against her own, stunning her. She moans and relaxes. In its crib the baby stirs and begins to coo. As he tears the woman's nightgown from her thighs, he hears the baby gurgling in the dark. The sound excites him.

Outside there is a sudden gust of icy wind. The sheet of oiled paper rises with a clatter into the air. The moon blazes; he sees his own socks rolling like tumbleweed across the room.

Grunting, he fumbles with his buckle, undoes the clasp, and tugs the belt free. Bucking wildly, the woman still pinned beneath him, he manages to kick off his other boot and lower his pants. He tears her nightgown open at the throat with his teeth and bites into a dewy breast. His mouth fills with milk as sweet as cream.

As the baby burbles in its crib, Twitty's prick writhes against the woman's belly like a decapitated snake. Whinnying victory, he opens the sluices and enters her.

Twitty slides upstream. The woman is a torrent; she inundates the floor. They are thrashing in a deep pool. He hears the baby's busy murmur, a bubbling like a happy brook beside them. The woman smells of scented rushes.

As Twitty's oar swells, his body shrinks into its blade of pleasure, a throbbing boat rowing in the woman's swollen creek. Like the dead man's saddle, she is enormous. Twitty is swimming. The baby is blowing bubbles, whiffling, guggling, percolating, and jumping up and down. Could be he's egging them on.

When in the bleary darkness overhead Twitty perceives the mummy and the smiling skeleton, it is too late. For although his testicles turn to ice and his reed shrivels like a witch in water, Twitty has been sucked into the vortex like a fly. The shack heaves and shudders. There is a sound like a hiccup and a belch. Something like gleet seeps out from under the door. Outside, all about, their many feet still as stones, the many temple sweepers are listening.

Aunt Rose and Uncle Friedle

When Uncle Friedle came back from the wars he had left his head behind him in a potato field somewhere north of Dover. Aunt Rose said jokingly to my mother that it didn't matter much—she had not married Friedle for his brains but for the jack-in-the-box he carried between his thighs. This must have been so—they lived happily together for over thirty years, though I often heard Rose complain that Uncle Friedle didn't eat enough.

Rose made up for Uncle Friedle's lack of appetite by eating like a horse herself. A woman of great energy, she spent most of the day in the kitchen skinning eels, steaming dumplings, jamming onions and clotted blood into vast iridescent mountains of intestines, rolling marzipan and meatballs in her fat hands. Her hands—bewitched bouquets of pig sausage—were always in motion; poking around in the batter, reaching for a marrow bone in the soup, testing the fullness of a fig, the firmness of a banana, the freshness of a slice of cake. And because Friedle turned up his nose at all these good things she—a fat and desperate pelican—settled down at the table to eat everything herself.

Soon she was of such gigantic proportions that Friedle had to stand up on the kitchen table if he wanted to fuck her, while she, spread across the stove, rose and fell like a monumental yeast loaf. And the day came when she was so gross that his jack could not find her box and Rose took Friedle tenderly between her teeth like one of the sweet and succulent blood sausages of which she was so particularly fond, to drink him down like a festive pint of ale.

When Rose could no longer move about freely and was forced to remain seated for fear her heart would burst its fatty socket, Friedle made for her a comfortable rocker in which she spent most of her life cheerfully sticking walnuts into the fudge.

One day Rose was preparing coleslaw. As she was about to slice into a large head of cabbage a smile spread across her dimpled face like jam. That night as Friedle lay fast asleep, Rose sewed the cabbage onto his neck with some fine bleached catgut. When Friedle woke up the next morning he was very angry with Rose, but she said:

"It's a fine head, Friedle, better than the one you lost." Friedle relented and grew a mustache.

As soon as Uncle Friedle had a head, his appetite came back. He even out-ate Aunt Rose and she—with less food on her plate —popped out of her rocker like a chestnut from its skin. They took to taking walks, Rose smiling and clutching the knockwurst with one hand and Friedle with the other.

One day after a hearty picnic of meatballs, pressed duck, stuffed goose, jam patties, pretzels, apple tart, gingerbread, and goose liver, Aunt Rose and Uncle Friedle fell asleep in the grass under a hazelnut tree. While they were sleeping a large white rat came by and fell in love with Friedle's head. He ate all of it but for the mustache which he took home to his wife as a gift. Rose woke up first and when she saw that Uncle Friedle had lost his head for a second time, she scribbed a note of adieu on a greasy piece of brown paper and ran off to marry a fancy haberdasher whom she had refused thirty years before.

When Friedle awoke and found himself alone he reached deep inside his vest pocket and took out his head which he had safely kept wrapped up in a handkerchief all those years. Then he put it on backwards—something he had often done in private—and aiming a small revolver at his temple blew out his brains.

The second before the lights went out Friedle tried to think of Rose spread across the stove. But her image would not be summoned and instead he saw the tender kidneys of a quartered rabbit suspended between flesh and bone in their silvery membrane like the bull's grey testicles that he had seen that morning hanging free in the butcher's stall.

La Chincha

It is morning. In its cage the parakeet greedily husks seeds.

"Tell me a story, *abuelita* Emelina," I beg, settling myself into the bruised couch. "A *good* story."

"I'll tell you the one about the chocolate factory in Cuba. The one about the man who gets his finger mashed in the machinery and they have to throw all the chocolate out."

"I know it already. *Please*. Another one."

My father's mother sighs and scratches the corner of her mouth.

"All right. I'll tell the story of the little girl with the small white hands who wants to stroke the lion at the zoo. 'We'll go to the zoo and see the big lion,' her mother says, 'if you promise—' "

"No! Oh, Lina! *Mi querida*. I know that one too. You've told it so often! Please—I want a new story."

"A story I have never told before?"

"Yes!"

"Not to you or anyone else? You won't repeat it to your mother? *Me prometes?*"

"Cross my heart. Cross my heart and hope to *die!*"

My grandmother looks me over carefully. Pleased with what she sees, she sucks on her teeth with satisfaction.

"Sophia, my princess—tomorrow you are nine. I will tell you the story of *La Chincha*." She sits back, prods her breasts, folds her fat speckled arms across her belly, clucks at the parakeet, and begins:

"Once I was very beautiful. As beautiful as you will be, *hijita*. Men brought me gifts of fruit-ices and roses the color of summer butter. They clowned and made lovesick faces when I walked down the street. I had a green silk dress—it clung to my body like a vine. Ah! But the story is not about me, I am forgetting!"

She laughs and pulls her matted robe down over her naked knees.

"I knew a girl, a shameful girl—cheap and reckless—a piece of trash! Though I was a queen, she was pretty too. The men called her *La Chincha*—the bedbug—because of the way she jumped around. A dirty slut with yellow hair and a purple mouth. Always running after men. Always jumping in and out of bed!" She illustrates her story with a gesture of the hand and, bending over, whispers huskily:

"Always lying under the staircase at the Havana Botanical Gardens! Panting like a bitch in heat! Legs spread wide apart!"

"Why, Lina? What was she doing?"

"She had nothing on under her dress! Naked as an egg!"

"Oh! No! Not *really*! But why?"

"She was sick! A sick slut! Her sickness is called *furor uterine!*"

"What does it mean?"

"Cunt on fire! Her cunt was on fire! Burned her alive!"

"Cunt?" I am astounded by this word I have never heard. "*Cunt?*"

"Her *sex*, little fool! Her vulva! ON FIRE! BURNED HER ALIVE! She caught men under that staircase. A regular Venus's-flytrap! They could smell her a mile away. They said she needed *twenty men a day* to put out her fire!" She slaps her thighs and sits back triumphantly. Catching her excitement, the parakeet scrabbles up and down its perch and shits.

✳

In the evening I go back to her, a dish of ice cream in my hand and the shy request that has been eating its way into my head for hours:

"The story, *abuelita* Emelina. The story about the one they called *La Chincha*. I want to hear it. Again."

Desire

No, there is no magic. The face puckers like a fig forgotten in the tree; the features screw into a fist. The hours eat with such voracity! Deadly incisors that lengthen with the passage of time.

Sophia, my little one, my pretty one, be kind to this moldering fruit, this blighted root. I wasn't born an old woman. But tumbled into the world as fragrant as those golden lemons twinkling in the trees. Ah! We are all born princesses only to shrivel in the sun, sister sticks too soon heaped together, fodder for the writhing kine of Death. The future isn't tremendous, let me tell you! Laugh at my breasts like yams, my flesh that hangs from my spine like dead meat from a hook! Once I was like the fig tree, pliable and green.

When I was just sixteen, my own grandmother sent me a ruby from Ciego de Avila and a pair of green leather sandals. They lay coupled like wet lizards in their box. Red, the ruby whispered arson; green, the shoes spoke of subversion, and I, resolved not to be the prey of some well-oiled bureaucrat of my father's acquaintance, stole that very night past the snoring hounds who slept before my father's door, slid down the waxed oak banister, and ran naked to the beach. I was hungry for a lover and wanted no other than the Master of the Sea himself—the one we called Pescado Verón. Since infancy I'd known his name and dreamed of his deep coral kingdoms. I stood in the surf certain to see him, horned and finned, a weedy staff stiffly glowing in his hand.

Ah! Little tease! Don't think I miss your cruel grin! What of it if he was not there? If I waited, my heart suspended on the salty wind for the greater part of the starry night? Listen: at dawn a little boat leapt to the horizon; from the beach I saw it approach bobbing like a cork, my throat and my feet blinking a signal: one red, two green; one red, two green—calling the fisherman to shore.

You have stopped laughing? The little slut grows warm! It seems the old hag's tale is not without charm after all. Is that your heart I see fluttering beneath your breast or is a fish agonizing there? Do you see the little boat, its paint the color of his eyes but flaking, green scabs sliding into the sea to be swallowed by black turtles and foam? Do you see his eyes dancing like candles when he sees her waiting and wonders what it is shining at her throat—is it blood, a witchy wound? Is she a ghost, a dead girl haunting the coast in her burial shoes? And having trapped a thousand-thousand shiny souls in his silver net, he wonders at the tricks of Fate and, choosing blindness, bites her hook.

He slips into the water and his body is outlined against the white sky; the faded cloth clings to him as he wades towards her. He pulls the boat to shore and leaves it secure upon the rocks; there is salt in his hair and skin; she knows his mouth will taste of salt and longs as horses long to lick the white slabs humped and half hidden on the grassy hill. She knows his fingers will burn her, that their smoky alphabet will leave marks.

He approaches her in silence. His smile is a cliff bearded with wild thyme, craggy and difficult to climb. He says nothing but falls to his knees and with his tongue opens her throbbing shell. Soon her only desire is to climb his tree and fell him and of his wood make paper kites to set her love sailing across the sky—

Paper kites, windborne and fragile, as fragile as an old woman's heart, Sophia, and—like an old woman's desire—inflammable in the heat of a summer's morning.

Saida

for Salman Rushdie

I recall that on the professor's desk, a scarlet beetle levitated upon its pin. And that as he scolded his daughter Saida, I fixed the beetle with my eyes so as not to give myself away for a coward and a fool by weeping or laughing.

Her crime was this: she had seized me by the wrist and together we had trespassed within the confines of her father's study. Here Saida revealed a terrible mystery: a two-headed cobra, taken in Luxor, and bottled.

Saida had placed the snake on a small table in full sunlight in order to impress me and so master my heart. Although my heart was already hers; only an hour before, in a chamber as cluttered as a tomb, and as I lay napping beside her in a bed cocooned with mosquito netting, she had touched me with candor and fire, pressed her mouth to mine, taken my tongue between her teeth—so that I fell at once into a species of swoon, the bed spinning in a fiery orbit. For hours we breathed a turbulent air.

The air within the professor's forbidden room was turbulent, too, and the snake was hot: it glowed in its keeping medium like a glass wand in a kiln.

＊

Much of Saida's mystery had evolved from conversations shared throughout her unique childhood with her father. She knew of a tribe beyond Egypt's southmost border that included in its totemic system the boiled bones of meat, sexual passion, and the color blue. These people tattooed their faces and the backs of their hands with blue zoological series; the tattoos were simultaneously prestigious and magical.

These things I had learned from Saida the very first time we spoke together in the school gardens, after she had teased me for wearing a Koran as a charm, prodding it disdainfully. It dangled between a teapot the size of a thumbtack and with an articulated lid, and a tiny Turk's slipper. I told her the bracelet had belonged to my mother.

My father was a missionary, and I had been nurtured with the poisoned milk of his own thwarted desires. Malevolence, in father's fevered view, was ubiquitous, yet lacked specific definition, so that the world was jinxed by a multiplicity of prohibitions and temptations; everything of intensity—pleasure and pain, beauty and ugliness, the bitter and the sweet—seduced me equally.

The instant Saida's knowing finger touched me, the room, at once diurnal and nocturnal, and reflecting us as might a necromancer's mirror of molten lead, was itself become so hot it is a wonder our shoes, abandoned on the floor, did not burst into flame—

As had the shoes of a classmate whose home had caught fire; her shoes had saved her. Awakening to the sound of them hissing on the roasting floor, she had screamed.

Until Egypt, my knowledge of fire was academic. Those shoes transmuting to ash upon the floor, and my soul burning in Saida's embrace, revealed fissures reaching into the world's wild center—as would her father's treasures, yet unseen, cooking in the shadows.

I have said that Saida had placed the canopic bottle on a small table the better to see it. If, as we gazed upon it, Saida had not embraced me, nothing would have happened. But she reached out suddenly and clasped me, and we fell together, knocking the little table over. As the table disclosed four claws and four brass balls, the snake tumbled from its shattered glass. A fine old book entitled *Coleoptera of the Sahara* fell also. Sopping up the keeping medium, its green leather binding veered to pink. The rug, too, was discolored by the snake's bathwater.

Later that night, alone in a room furnished only with a bed and a Bible, I remember thinking that Saida and I were like the snake: two-headed and joined as a woman and a man (and it was Saida who had informed me of this joining). Our fictive fucking was as potent as a life-giving venom, an intoxication.

Only because Saida's father was such a distinguished figure did mine allow those weekly visits. The professor's study roiled with a multitude of queerly beautiful things, and my father had warned me that the contemplation of nature was evil. God's world was not to be scrutinized. It contained, by a cosmic error he could not explain, or would not, a pervasive evil.

In other words, if one looked too closely at a thing, one risked finding oneself eye to eye with the Prince of Darkness. As when looking too long at one's reflection one might see something hellish within one's own face; large doses of a smooth mirror could reveal the soul's fractures. (Navigated in a silence suggesting illness, our house was mirrorless. It contained no treasure nor luxury.)

And if Saida's love had revealed a fracture of another sort, a precipice of which I had no previous knowledge, the fire that had reduced the hotel to a black smear had revealed a fracture in the earth and the mummified body of a girl, her bandages seeded with symbols of potencies: little clay figures glazed blue.

✺

The professor scolded his daughter, all the while looking at me. And because I continued to stare at the beetle—pinned through the scutellum and swimming in air—having chosen that point in space as a mooring for my soul which was pitching under the impulse of an uncertain weather—he laughed. His laughter was engaging, informed by an acute intelligence. He asked: "Are you *curious?*" Eagerly, I nodded. He turned and, taking a key from his pocket, opened an ebony cabinet faced with polished plate glass, where I saw the snake suspended anew in an identical jar. Smelling of camphor, the room was all at once cordial and ceremonial.

"In Egypt, once," he said, "very long ago, certain mystics insisted that it was feminine curiosity that precipitated the world." He pointed out two deep chairs. Expectant and relieved, Saida and I sat in that room where a thousand creatures were kept; a place that was, like Saida's bed, simultaneously diurnal and nocturnal.

First the professor pulled forth boxes two inches deep and tightly covered with glass. Here infinitesimal insects gummed to mica triangles glowed like elements in a vast chain of mythical associations: the corporealization of a lunar dew, the corneas of wizards, the lenses of another world. Next, settled deeper, were locusts—some surprisingly large and looking like the sacred vessels of a diminutive royalty. There were spiders also; the professor pointed out their mouths and multiple eyes. One was so enormous it could have been worn on the head of a child in guise of a velvet hat, a ceremonial hat sewn for an initiation into the darkest rites of the natural world, rites which my father had refused to name and number, but which I now know are numberless—and finite, too, for even as I write this, the world dies and the blue seeds of afterlife are only a sterile clay, after all.

Next, the professor showed us bottled fetuses, some like featureless lumps of wax, except that when looking closer I saw the finlike hands and the faces on the verge of forming. There were eggs in quantity—yellow, black, and blue; some were shaped like tops and some like whistles and one—the egg of a cuttlefish, I believe—looked like a corkscrew.

This cornucopic display thrust Saida and me into such a state of fearlessness that later, in the blackening penumbra of her room, we lit a candle and took it under the sheets. It gilded us. Saida's vulva, as fuzzy as a peach, was crimson there where the fruit was sweetly incised. And it seemed, in those final hours when our mouths fused together and we sobbed with delight, that the *khamsin* raged within the room, that the air was a living wind in which bright things by the thousands agitated their wings.

✻

Even years later, long after our fathers had cruelly fought and I was denied access to those rooms upon which a slip of the tongue had incurred malediction (in anger I had revealed that

I had seen how even tyrants begin their lives as fish; how the world had not formed in seven days but, instead, slowly, painfully), I could feel Saida's mouth—the mouth of Venus Matutina, Venus Vesputina—pressed to the secret cipher between my legs, and I would fall back, as into the celestial void, and hear the stars tearing past, shredding the fabric of the night.

Voyage to Ultima Azul, Chapter 79

> The Gods, kin to spiders, have eyes that like crowns circumvent their heads. Thus they see everything (but can be tricked by an inspired gesture be it quick enough—and there is your freedom, your cunning escape hatch—trick the spider and break the jealous web of destiny! Through the tear perceive other worlds, other ways!).
>
> —from the *Terra Uta Codex*

And so we had at last torn *Astral UVA*—that embattled and embittered ship—from the dark and viscous clasp of space as ravenous of flesh as of metal, of machines as of men—

She dropped, her ribs fissured, and we tucked beneath, our hearts like moons thudding in the crazy void above our heads, conjuring the tough outer rind to hold fast—that festering amalgam of sulfurous malachite, supraplastics and bone, pitted, pocketed, and bruised, fingered by time and raped by battle, as mottled as an overripe banana penetrating trackless distances—now steadily approaching the faceless sphere, featureless name: Ultima Azul—already a pinprick in a skein of silk, stretched, stained, torn, dyed, knotted, folded, washed, worn—by what gods? Benevolent? Asleep? Blind? Hostile?

We gained upon her, now a sequin scintillating, and not a moment too soon. For as we hurtled towards that mysterious world (perhaps only to perish in the giant gullet of some unforeseeable disaster: mammoth crab, reptile, or spider, greedy paw of famished cyclops, foaming cunt of Panty Deity, new volcano, sea of nitric acid, bubbling mudbath, oozing quicksand) our ship began to break up, spitting pieces of itself as a man with a mashed face spits teeth, shedding its fretted crust of solder, silver, nails, and scales like fur. Would we get there in time? Would we come to a world hung like an egg in a sock, palpitating beneath a jungle as tightly woven and as impenetrable as those hideous forests of the Grandling Ur, its spiteful moons Glower and Sink? And if there was an atmosphere and a place wide enough, smooth, and solid enough to take the crushing weight of the ship, would she maneuver now as she had in the past—mangled and bleeding as she was after that foul encounter with the fiendish scorpion-men of Goar? How steady the hands of Captain Rigor? How clear the head of his first mate Lurid? Both had been battered, tried and torn in the thick and thin of travel, caught for months like moths in a cosmic circus that like a great scream coiled—a labyrinthine bowel in the belly of Time.

Rigor's wound—a feverish seism across his heart—still festered despite the holographic skin graft, and Lurid's eyes still filled with blood at the slightest allusion to the Bay of Dim, its twin-brained, twin-cocked Master of Misery-Glower. . . .

Steadily we approached this uncharted orb that blinked and beckoned to us like the eye of a parrot from within a black tree, and with a shudder entered her atmosphere, thin at first, no more than a subtle perfume wafting from between two fragrant breasts from a far corner of a great room, and then thickening, greening, dense and acrid, speaking to us of a planet pubescent, anxious, and warm; of forests rooting above blind rivers of seething lava, of excited seas raging with new appetites. A virgin world then, of seeds untested, of restless dreams, of whispered promises.

We sped into this florid air heaving, engines gasping, laboring in sickness and longing; now perceived her husk—ripping through her nimbus, her cirrocumulus as through petticoats— and she raised herself to greet us, showing round and youthful contours, flushed and joyful. A lonely planet, but coy and playful, pleased with our gift of tortured metal, our hunger for her fruits, her clay, her gases. A world generous in furry grottoes, hills and hollows, secret coves, birds (we saw them now), therefore berries, perhaps bees—

And then, at the flank of a mossy mountain glowing in the fire of her twin suns, *we saw a place to land:* a flat pelvic thrust of bedrock jutting out to sea (a sea brimming with ovum, caught in the quick of stunning metamorphosis, its bouquets of plankton spitting secrets into the surf, the countless brittle bodies of starfish shimmering on the weedy surface woven of reed, leaf, shell, and seed) and we fell to the ground, the motors screaming victory, the ship in frenzied success chewing itself to bits: cogs, cables, acids, and teeth ground out in a final feast, all parts self-consuming, metals fusing with glass, rare ethers galvanized, wires and magnets now sticky pools, scorched powders. The stench of conflagration—boiling oils, of rubber and celluloid mating, cornucopias of incandescences, of embers, the terrible soup of acetone stirred with bile—of a machine in the jaws of Death. The *Astral UVA* would never sail again. But as the dense smoke billowed through the stairwells, smashed capsules, and cells, we came to a shuddering halt. And as the mutant children wept with joy, the few baboons, frogs, and cats that had survived the voyage clamored their satisfaction, the hull split open like a fruit, its great ragged mouth gaped helplessly at the sky it had vanquished, mangled but victorious, fused to rock forever.

Sleepers awaking, our grey flesh tingling beneath the warm tongues of sister suns, the old dreams stirred; our blood flowed fast now, darkening, already inventing a new language for Desire.